Praise for *Of Mice and Minestrone*

"An absolute treasure trove for Hap and Leonard fans. Going back to the beginning only deepens our love and appreciation for these guys. This collection proves once again why Joe Lansdale is one of our very best."
—Ace Atkins, author of *The Shameless*

"*Of Mice and Minestrone* is the last bit of connective tissue missing from the Hap and Leonard Mythos, which is one of the most entertaining series in modern literature. This book, which deals with abuse, friendship, violence, growing up, race, food, and justice, is full of the wit that's made Lansdale a star."
—Gabino Iglesias, author of *Coyote Songs*

"Five stories, four of them new, filling in more of the early years of that imperishable East Texas duo, Hap Collins and Leonard Pine. Kathleen Kent's brief introduction suggests that the running theme here is 'Kindness and Cruelty.' An even more precise motto might be 'Violence Is Inevitable,' since Lansdale consistently treats the often lethal outbursts of his characters in disarmingly matter-of-fact terms, as if the boys couldn't help it . . . laden with the same irresistible combination of relaxed badinage and playful threats that sometimes spiral into serious consequences while still remaining playful. The 17 down-home recipes contributed by Lansdale's daughter, Kasey, many of them as chatty as the stories, are a bonus."
—*Kirkus*

"There's a place in East Texas where story shades into memory, where violence and tenderness are just part of the wonder

of living, and that's precisely where Joe Lansdale lives, and writes from, and we're all the better for it. The eating's pretty good there, too, as Hap's recipes more than attest. You leave this book hungry, both for food and to start the whole series all over again, live through it one more time, maybe just live there a while."
—Stephen Graham Jones, author of *Mongrels*

"In these character studies of his two most charismatic protagonists, Joe Lansdale takes us to the dark side of Mayberry—authentic tales of small town life in the heart of the twentieth century that also provide an unflinching look at the violence that charged the last gasps of Jim Crow, with all the force of the Sabine River at flood stage."
— Christopher Brown, author of *Tropic of Kansas*

Praise for Joe R. Lansdale

"A folklorist's eye for telling detail and a front-porch raconteur's sense of pace."
—*New York Times Book Review*

"A terrifically gifted storyteller."
—*Washington Post Book Review*

"Like gold standard writers Elmore Leonard and the late Donald Westlake, Joe R. Lansdale is one of the more versatile writers in America."
—*Los Angeles Times*

"A zest for storytelling and gimlet eye for detail."
—*Entertainment Weekly*

"Lansdale is an immense talent."
—*Booklist*

"Lansdale is a storyteller in the Texas tradition of outrageousness . . . but amped up to about 100,000 watts."
—*Houston Chronicle*

"Lansdale's been hailed, at varying points in his career, as the new Flannery O'Connor, William Faulkner-gone-madder, and the last surviving splatterpunk . . . sanctified in the blood of the walking Western dead and righteously readable."
—*Austin Chronicle*

Praise for *Hap and Leonard: Blood and Lemonade*

"*Blood and Lemonade* is the best of Lansdale and the best of Hap and Leonard. As urgent as it is timeless. As fun as it is thoughtful. It haunts you while it kicks your ass. Joe never lets you down, just shows you over and over why he's the best."
—Jim Mickle, director of *Cold in July*

"A brilliant 'mosaic' novel. An amazingly vivid style that feels like Hemingway. Themes that are especially important for our time. With these early adventures of his compelling Hap and Leonard characters, Joe R. Lansdale hits a new high."
—David Morrell, *New York Times* bestselling author of *Murder as a Fine Art*

"Magnificent storytelling."
—*Char's Horror Corner*

Selected works by Joe R. Lansdale

Hap and Leonard

Savage Season (1990)
Mucho Mojo (1994)
The Two-Bear Mambo (1995)
Bad Chili (1997)
Rumble Tumble (1998)
Veil's Visit: A Taste of Hap and Leonard (with Andrew Vachss, 1999)
Captains Outrageous (2001)
Vanilla Ride (2009)
Hyenas (2011)
Devil Red (2011)
Dead Aim (2013)
Honky Tonk Samurai (2016)
Hap and Leonard (2016)
Rusty Puppy (2017)
Coco Butternut (2017)
Blood and Lemonade (2017)
The Big Book of Hap and Leonard (2018)
Jack Rabbit Smile (2018)
The Elephant of Surprise (2019)

Other novels

Act of Love (1981)
Dead in the West (1986)
The Magic Wagon (1986)
The Nightrunners (1987)
The Drive-In (1988)
Cold in July (1989)
Tarzan: the Lost Adventure (1995) (with Edgar Rice Burroughs)
The Boar (1998)
Freezer Burn (1999)
Waltz of Shadows (1999)
The Big Blow (2000)
The Bottoms (2000)
A Fine Dark Line (2002)
Sunset and Sawdust (2004)
Lost Echoes (2007)
Leather Maiden (2008)
Flaming Zeppelins (2010)
All the Earth, Thrown to Sky (2011)
Edge of Dark Water (2012)
The Thicket (2013)
Paradise Sky (2015)
Fender Lizards (2015)
Bubba and the Cosmic Blood-Suckers (2017)
Terror Is Our Business (2018) (with Kasey Lansdale)

OF MICE AND MINESTRONE

HAP AND LEONARD THE EARLY YEARS

JOE R. LANSDALE

TACHYON
SAN FRANCISCO

Tachyon Publications LLC
1459 18th Street #139
San Francisco, CA 94107
www.tachyonpublications.com
tachyon@tachyonpublications.com

Series Editor: Jacob Weisman
Editor: Rick Klaw

Printed in the United States of America by Versa Press, Inc.

Print ISBN: 978-1-61696-323-1
Digital ISBN: 978-1-61696-324-8

First Edition: 2020
9 8 7 6 5 4 3 2 1

For my niece Pamela Lansdale Dunklin,
lady of many talents

CONTENTS

INTRODUCTION

KATHLEEN KENT

WESTERN WRITER J. FRANK DOBIE said at the beginning of his novel *Coronado's Children*, "These tales are not creations of mine. They belong to the soil and to the people of the soil." Joe R. Lansdale, one of the most prolific and natural-born storytellers I've ever known, seems to summon up his far-ranging narratives not so much from the heady ether of the Literary Muses, but from the Martian-red dirt of East Texas.

He's written at least forty-five novels, thirty short story collections, many chapbooks and comic book adaptations, but while I've spent several weeks reading this newest collection of early Hap and Leonard stories, *Of Mice and Minestrone*, there's a good chance he's published even more. Some of Joe's awards include ten Bram Stoker Awards, a British Fantasy Award, an Edgar Award for *The Bottoms*, and a World Horror Convention Grand Master Award. There are many other awards, both national and international. He's been inducted into the Texas Literary Hall of Fame, and several of his novels and short stories have been adapted to film.

I'd already been a fan of his, especially of his darkly majestic novel *The Bottoms*, but I'd never met him until we were on book tour together and at the Texas Book Festival in Austin. We shared the same publisher, and he'd just launched *Rusty Puppy*, number twelve in the Hap and Leonard series. I found to my delight that his growing up in East Texas mirrored a lot of my own childhood experiences, including the Piney Woods lexicon of Guns, God, and Grits (and usually in that order). Shared also was the frequently challenging work of rising out of the black tar of, as Joe would put it, "not being poor, just broke," and of subsequently being rescued by books, reading, and writing.

This new collection of Hap and Leonard stories takes the duo back to their youth, and illuminates, on a very personal level, the origins of their friendship. Sometimes painful, sometimes hilarious, the stories may not be completely autobiographical, but there is a strong thread of authenticity in the development of Joe's characters. The people he writes about who inhabit the sometimes-fictional towns behind the Pine Curtain *feel* real. The reader loves Hap and Leonard because Joe Lansdale loves them. They bleed, and sweat, and make love, and do actual work. And even the most despicable of the villains in the series are lovingly drawn, even if they are developed with a very dark, nightmarish ink.

A lot of Joe Lansdale's writing, whether it be western-themed, science fiction, or contemporary crime, is violent. He has the soul of a poet, but he's also a realist and understands the often-confounding truth of living behind the Pine Curtain. "In East Texas," Joe has said, "there's a kindness and a violence that's like a two-edged sword. You can find the kindest, most hospitable people here—and they'll shoot you over what I might think of as a mere slight."

If there is one theme running through all the Hap and Leonard stories within this collection, it might be "Kindness and Cruelty." The tension throughout the narratives is not *if* the violence will erupt, but *when*. In "Sparring Partner" a boxing coach named Dixie says to Hap, "Leonard would make a hell of a boxer . . . Could go all the way. And you too, except you got a streak of kindness in you." That streak of kindness does not in any way prevent Hap, however, from beating someone's ass when the occasion calls for it.

There is a strong sense of the moral "rightness" of things that seems inherent in both Hap and Leonard, even if—as is illustrated in the title story, "Of Mice and Minestrone," where Hap tries to rescue a battered woman—no good deed goes unpunished. But there is no preciousness, no sentimentality to these moral corrections from the two friends, and often the lesson is learned through the criminal's blood, sweat, and tears.

The stories are redolent with details of growing up in East Texas, a place that is not really the South, and not really like the rest of Texas. The weather is hot and humid, the vegetation lush, the spiders and snakes venomous, the women often more so. But Joe Lansdale's true genius lies in revealing his characters' strengths and weaknesses through dialogue—sometimes sparse, sometimes loquacious, but always true to the time and place. And, often, the simplest dialogue addresses the most weighted social issues, like racial injustice, sexual and family violence, and the repercussions of fighting in foreign wars. In the story "The Sabine Was High," Leonard talks about his time in Viet Nam: "You know, I'd be lying there in the jungle . . . and I could hear people praying, but I didn't pray, because, like you, I'm not a believer . . . But I damn sure believed in hope then, because that's all I had to believe in, except being ready."

These stories deepen and enrich the already iconic standing of the Hap and Leonard series. Although, the adventures are new, they all feel as comfortable and familiar as a long-anticipated homecoming. As Hap says, "There are some people you don't talk to for a couple years, maybe more, and soon as you see them, it's like they have only left the room for a moment, and that's how it was with me and Leonard."

Kathleen Kent
http://www.kathleenkent.com

HAP AND LEONARD, THE EARLY DAYS

Hap and Leonard have been with me a long time, and since their source comes from the well of my experience, in another way they have been with me even longer.

I have enjoyed writing about them over the years, and they are without a doubt my favorite character creations. I might have written some stand-alone books that will register higher on the critical meter, but the characters and their conflicts and adventures have gone on steadily to my delight, and gratefully, to the equal delight of the readers.

This book is a collection of short stories written about the duo in their early years. In the TV show *Hap and Leonard* they met as children, but that was TV. In my world they met later, as teenagers, and it wasn't until they were young men out of high school, one coming back from prison, the other from the Vietnam War, that their friendship was solidified to the status of brothers.

A previous volume, *Blood and Lemonade*, deals with this meeting in a story titled "Tire Fire." The stories in that book deal mostly with Hap and his parents, and some with Leonard, and they are all tied together by a connecting tissue that is a kind of story unto itself.

I had great fun writing those stories, as I did with these. Here Hap and Leonard are together much more, and as the stories continue, they are about the both of them. Navigating their world, growing tough and, in Hap's case, disappointed in love (hinted at) and in his lifetime ambitions.

There are other stories about the pair I may eventually tell. I've wanted to write about Hap's meeting with Trudy and how he chose to go to prison to protest the draft, and how Trudy, who encouraged him to do just that, abandoned him while he was behind bars, sent him divorce papers. But that story is yet to come.

The first story, "The Kitchen," more of a vignette really, sets the tone for who Hap was, and the last story sets the tone for who he has become. "The Sabine Is High" deals with the aftermath of Hap's marriage and his time in prison, and at the same time deals with Leonard's return from Viet Nam, and how they both have some heavy experiences to deal with, which may in ways explain at least some of their penchant for righting wrongs and dealing with both the light and the darkness in their souls.

HAP AND LEONARD, THE EARLY DAYS

One thing that is unique about this volume is not just a few stories were written for it, rounded out with already published stories. This volume contains only one story that has been previously published, "The Watering Shed," and all the others appear here for the very first time, and currently this is the only place you can read them.

Another unique element is the recipes. They are inspired by the food mentioned in the stories, and my daughter Kasey provides those. We thought they might be a fun addition, since food is important to the Hap and Leonard stories, the same as music.

I hope you enjoy reading these stories as much as I enjoyed writing them.

And so, from the wilds of East Texas, I bid you adieu.

Joe R. Lansdale
Nacogdoches, Texas
June 2019

THE KITCHEN

I MUST HAVE BEEN SIX or seven at the time, and it was an event that went on for years, this gathering of relatives. Neither do I remember the occasion, or if there was one. Meaning it had nothing to do with Christmas, Thanksgiving, or any holiday. I believe it was just a visit to Grandma's house. She lived about an hour from us, in a big old house on about thirty acres. She was quite old then, but still very mobile. She was the only living grandparent I had. The others had died long ago.

My grandmother had been born in the 1880s and had come to Texas as a child in a covered wagon from Oklahoma Territory. She had seen Buffalo Bill's Wild West Show, and she had seen men land on the moon. She lived to be nearly a hundred years old, until a bout of pneumonia killed her chance at achieving a centennial.

On this day it was cold. Not common in East Texas, but we have a couple, sometimes three months or so, when it's that way. It wasn't icy or wet, just cold.

The smell of chicken frying in lard after being dipped and rolled in flour and eggs and dropped into the hot grease was the smell that woke me up. I don't remember what day of the week it was, but my father wasn't there, so it was most likely a workday. That could be any day from Monday to Saturday, and sometimes on Sunday, though my mother and other religious folks didn't like the idea of working on the day of the Sabbath.

"Let God come get me," my dad used to say, and I could envision him whipping God's ass. My dad inspired a lot of confidence.

When I got up, my mother fixed me breakfast. I remember I had what she called cornmeal mush. It was essentially grits with butter and a tablespoon of sugar and a dash of milk. It was my favorite breakfast food at that age. Now and again I added a sliced banana.

While I ate, my mother dipped the fried chicken out of the deep skillet with tongs, and put it on a plate covered with paper towels, and then she covered the chicken in paper towels.

After my breakfast, I got to mix the cornbread batter with a wooden spoon so big and long I had to rest it on my shoulder. When that was done, she made cornbread in the oven, and then we packed everything in boxes and brown paper sacks to be loaded in the car. I don't know what kind of car it was, but it was green. She let me carry some mixing bowls and a sack that had some cooking utensils and a box of Lipton Tea, which most East Texans back then viewed as the nectar of the gods.

I still do.

Mama drove us to Grandma's house. Her house smelled of food, and I think it was then that food began to matter to me, not just to eat, but to smell and delight in.

No food has ever tasted as good to me again as the food our family shared.

Grandma's cooking smells were of dried pinto beans being made less dry, simmering on the stove. It was a gas stove, but there had been a wooden one in its place only a few years back. I had never seen her cook on that stove, it was before I was born, but the stove was in the barn out back. My uncle had pointed it out to me.

My grandmother lived with my uncles, and they had just begun to move into the present with a gas stove, and though they had electricity, kerosene lanterns were placed about the house and not too long back, my mother told me, that was all the light they had.

Other conveniences were to follow, though I remember drawing water up from the well in the backyard with a rope, bucket, and pulley. The only thing I hated about visiting my grandmother, and my uncles, was the outhouse. I hated the smell and the discomfort of sitting there in the heat waiting for a turd to pass, wiping my ass on magazine pages, a method that only slightly had the edge over dried oak leaves. Another worry was there always seemed to be a nest of wasps or yellow jackets in the corner of the ceiling.

My aunts from both sides of the family were there when we arrived, as well as my cousins, and I had a lot of them. We were close then, and saw each other frequently, but over the years moves and adulthood responsibilities had displaced us. At family gatherings we were close and played chase and hiding-go-seek outside while the grownups cooked and talked about bills and illness and a better job.

My grandmother had a huge table in her dining room just off the kitchen. She had photos framed on the wall of family members, living and dead. I remember one of my uncles when they were kids, standing with a goat between them. My Uncle Charlie leaned on crutches, his reward for having had polio. My Uncle Jimmy stood straight and tall with his chin slightly lifted. He had served in the Philippines during the war, and kind and gentle as he was, there were shadows in his eyes, and as I grew older, I knew why. He had been part of some of the hardest fighting that had occurred. Now, as an adult, I recognize those same shadows in my eyes, but for different reasons. And, from time to time I see and recognize the darkness lurking in the eyes of my best friend and brother Leonard.

As time for supper neared, the cooked food was pulled from the stovetop and oven, and the already cooked goods were re-warmed. I was told to go out to the smokehouse and fill a large straw basket with potatoes. The potatoes were kept in burlap bags, and on the opposite side of the log-and-lumber shack meat hung, cool and snug, smelling of salt and hickory smoke.

I was always unnerved to go out there. I had seen those hogs alive earlier that year and had patted one on the head. I wondered if that hog was one of those that was split and cured, hanging from a rafter with his friends and family.

I dug around in the bags and filled the basket with red potatoes. I was about to leave, when a long chicken snake slid out of the stack of potato bags and decided to stop right in front of the closed door, the smokehouse's only exit.

I knew from experience it was a chicken snake. We had a chicken house out back of our house, and we had rows of chickens there who laid eggs in straw-lined boxes. A few times, when I had gone with my father or mother to gather eggs, I had been startled by the same sort of snake. But I had my parents with me then, and my mother always kept an old hoe inside the door for just such incidents. Chicken snakes ate eggs and baby chicks, and we ate eggs too, so it was a survival of the fittest.

I didn't have my parents and I didn't have a hoe, but I had a chicken snake and a closed door. I decided I had to make it move, so I took potatoes from my basket and threw them at the snake. Frightened, it rose up and extended itself, its body cocked to strike. I didn't know then a chicken snake wasn't poisonous. All snakes were venomous in my view. I had heard tales that snakes could bite their tail and roll downhill like a wheel. I had heard of milk snakes that latched on to the udders of cows and sucked their milk. I heard of snakes that could fly.

For me snakes were all a dangerous and mysterious breed of crawling critter. Armed as I was with spuds, I continued to throw potatoes, and finally the snake zipped off, between the other lumpy potato bags. I raced to the door, and leaving it open as I stood just outside, I picked up the potatoes I had thrown, and put them back in the basket.

Rushing back to the house, I had my snake encounter to chatter about, hoping I would be rewarded for my bravery. Instead, my grandmother said, "Oh, that's Charlie. He's all right. He eats the rats that get in there."

My mother said, "Oh, I hate snakes. Even the rat eaters. I'm always reminded of the Adam and Eve story, and how the snake convinced Eve to eat the forbidden fruit."

"Charlie's all right," Grandma said. "I don't think he and the Bible snake are kin."

Some laughter went around, and then the women—my grandmother, mother, and aunts—reached into my basket of potatoes and sat in chairs placed in a circle with newspapers placed on the floor in front of them, and began to peel potatoes, the peelings dropping onto the paper, later to be tossed into the garden to naturally compost. The potato peeling went fast, and the potatoes were fried up fast in deep fryers of hot lard.

THE KITCHEN

Eventually my father and uncles showed up from work. My crippled Uncle Charlie came in on his crutches, and they all spoke to me and ruffled my hair, except my dad, who merely said, "Son."

Before long the food was all cooked, and the latest and strongest smell was off the French fries and pinto beans. With the recently cooked food, and the food brought for the event by the family, there was so much food one would have thought it was our plan to feed the local chapter of the National Guard.

It was all placed on long folding tables with folding metal chairs pushed up under them. All the kids were called in, and we all had to wash up. It was done in a big pan of water that was set into a basin, and we made a line in front of it that trailed into the living room. We took turns, and my Uncle Jimmy emptied the pan from time to time by standing in the backyard doorway, pushing the screen back, and tossing the water into the grass. He would then pour fresh water from the well bucket into the pan, and the line of hand washers would continue until we were all finished.

The youngsters' table and chairs were directly under the pin oak tree. We sat, and food was brought to us on plates. We didn't ask for anything in particular; the food was prepared for us, and there was no question of what we would eat.

We ate until we couldn't eat, and then the short day ended and the night came in, and with it the sounds of crickets, and the big bullfrogs down by the creek. Had it been the right time of year, the night would have been filled with fireflies.

A big metal oil drum with an opening cut into it set in the yard near the pin oak. It was stuffed with kindling and logs and the faint aroma of kerosene. It was lit by my Uncle Jimmy, and the fire licked out of the top and through rusted gaps throughout the barrel. The logs crackled, and the air several feet from the can was warmed.

When the food was eaten, the adults had coffee and the coffeepot was sat on top of the barrel to keep warm. And then came the sweets. My grandmother, mother, and aunts brought paper plates, cloth napkins, metal forks, and covered pies and cookies, German chocolate cake, which I hated, and thick but soft bricks of pecan bread. It all smelled wonderful. I zeroed in on my favorite: rich chocolate pie with high-mounded meringue.

These treats were stuffed into already full bellies, and in time my cousins wandered off to play chase in the dark, as was often done, and I played too, but soon I found myself back at the circle, listening to the adults. They were beginning to tell stories.

Stories of the Wild West Show, Billy the Kid, how my grandma and her kids had been so poor during the Depression that they had nothing to eat but a tow sack full of onions. And then my father told why he wouldn't eat mashed potatoes under any circumstances. As a child he had lived off of them for several months, potatoes being the only available food. He didn't care if they had butter on them, gravy, or were coated in bacon grease, the mere thought of them made him sick.

The stories dribbled out as it got late, and cars filled with the cousins, aunts, and uncles, and went away. We went away last, loading Mom's pans and plates and some of the leftovers into the back of her car. Every car had departed with leftovers.

Daddy went on ahead to the house in his work car, and we followed.

I sat in the back with the sacks of food, listened to pans and empty platters rattle in the trunk. I finally leaned against the car door. I could see bright stars in the clear night sky. I felt warm and sleepy.

The moon made the road in front of us shine, as if waxed. I drifted off. I dreamed of space travel like I had seen in the comic books or in the Buck Rogers and Flash Gordon serials on TV. I imagined I was a space captain, and my family always stocked my spaceship with home-cooked food before I started my space adventures with my trusty ray gun and extreme confidence. My spaceship, like those of Buck and Flash, spurted sparks and blossomed smoke, and the smoke ridiculously floated up.

Even dreaming, I smelled the aroma of fried chicken and pies and biscuits and cornbread. Smells of family gatherings and the warm kitchens where it was all cooked. The smells of contentment and security, all the grand things that a child adores before the illusion of magic and endless possibilities is broken by experience and time and life's plans tumble like meteors from the sky.

But in that moment, in that warm car with all those smells, I was as close to nirvana as a being could even be, or would ever be again.

OF MICE AND MINESTRONE

PART I

THAT SUMMER I got a job at the police station, which was also the city jail. These days a kid wouldn't be thought of for such a job, but back then it wasn't so uncommon, and a kid, like me, worked cheap.

It was in the little town of Marvel Creek, tucked tight in the East Texas pines, near the meandering brown river called the Sabine.

The police station was positioned near the center of town, and there were big oaks and massive pecan trees in the front yard, and it was cooler there in the summer than in a lot of places, because the trees had a nice shade. Inside the building it was comfortable too, because it was built of large blocks of granite and they stayed cool. There was an industrial-sized water cooler in one of the windows at the end of the hall, and if you came in during the dead of a hot summer day, it was pleasantly damp inside and the wind from the fan was enough to ruffle your hair.

I was sixteen then, and I was trying to make enough money to put gas in my car. My mother and father were far from well-to-do, but they had bought me a very fine used car, a bronze '64 Impala, and I thought I might actually start being able to date, taking a girl to the one theater in town, or driving her over to Tyler so we could go to movies there, or drive-in theaters, go out to eat, maybe just ride around, the evening culminating in a parking place somewhere that was romantic and quiet under a dark sky and bright stars.

The job made me feel older than my sixteen years. At the jail I heard a lot of cussing from inmates and cops, and that's where I stored up a lot of future verbal ammunition. There was one cop, Hilo Barnes, who I thought was exactly what a cop ought to be, just from the way he looked. The police department were all white guys, and wore uniforms, but the uniforms were tan and looked more like the sort a sheriff's crew would wear. They all had cowboy hats and .38 revolvers, and every man, for there were only men then, wore cowboy boots. All of them had blackjacks or slamjacks that they either carried in a back pocket or strapped to their gun belts. Hilo had dark sunglasses, and when you looked at him you could see yourself in them. He walked tall and had a kind of confidence that radiated off of him.

There were people behind the bars of the three cells

much of the time, and it was usually the same drunk who got hauled in on Friday night, and sometimes even voluntarily showed up to arrest himself, so that he might have a place to sleep it off. The other two usually held black prisoners who were in trouble for a variety of infractions, most often drunk and disorderly, fighting, and in a few cases certain things that were listed simply as "too uppity." Meaning that they had been acting too much like a white person, not strictly following the unwritten code that was the Jim Crow laws.

I would sweep and clean up and deliver meals to the prisoners, and most anything they needed there, and at the end of the week, on Friday, the eagle flew, as they used to say, meaning we were paid.

One late afternoon, not long after work, I stopped at a filling station on the way home. I pulled up at a pump with a car parked on the opposite side of it. A woman was sitting in the car on the passenger side, looking straight ahead, and the driver's side seat was empty.

Back then it was common for someone to come out and run your gas for you, wipe your windshield, check your oil and transmission fluid, make sure your tires had the right amount of air. It was part of the service.

But the station I stopped at was a one-man operation, and frequently the customers pumped their own gas, and paid afterward.

I got out of my car and got the pump going, put the gas nozzle in the tank, and started pumping. I didn't have enough money to fill the car up, but back then a dollar's gas would go a long way, even though it was almost as hard to come by as twenty dollars is today, maybe more.

The gas was pumped, and I went to hang up the nozzle, and as I did a bit of the gas inside of it splashed out, and as fate would have it, that's right when a burly, balding man stepped up to take the nozzle next, and some of the gas splashed on his boots.

The man said, "Goddamn, boy."

"Sorry, sir. I didn't mean to."

"You don't watch what you're doing."

"Sorry."

His face had turned red, and his shoulders looked tight under his loose-fitting black T-shirt, and he had rolled the T-shirt's short sleeves even shorter and tighter to show off his arms, which sported biceps only slightly smaller than a fat baby's head. He had on cuffed blue jeans and big black motorcycle boots that had almost seen their better days.

"Way to be more careful is to take an ass whipping, boy."

"I apologized, sir."

"Apology don't do my shoes no good, now does it?"

"No, sir, but it'll wipe off."

"That's the thing, boy. I shouldn't have to wipe them off at all. I think you're going to wipe them off, and you're going to do it with your shirttail."

"No, sir. I'm not going to do that."

He was bigger than me and no doubt more ruthless, but

even at sixteen I was stout and quick and had been training in boxing and wrestling and had just started training
in judo at the Tyler YMCA. I hadn't arrived at where I was
going to arrive in that training, but I had been in more
than a few fights, a couple of them of a serious survival nature, and I knew one damn thing for sure, I wasn't about
to wipe that asshole's shoes with my shirt, or anything else.

"I say you are going to do it."

That's when I heard the car door open, and the lady
got out and grabbed him by the arm and said, "Dash, he's
just a kid. He didn't mean nothing by it."

He turned his head slowly. It seemed dreamlike the
way he turned his head, and as he did I saw the woman
sort of sink inside herself and lift her hands, and then
the left hook came, and it knocked her hand aside and
caught her a solid one in the right eye. She staggered like
a drunk and fell back against the fender of the car and sat
down on the ground.

"You son of a bitch," I said, and right then the station
owner, Mr. Carlson, came out carrying a nightstick.

"Dash, now you go on, or I'll have to wrap this stick
around your head. Get your wife there, load her up, and
go on."

"You ought not get into my business," Dash said. "You
might end up with that thing stuck up your ass."

"Now, you go on. Get Minnie and go on. She may be
your business, but this place here, it's my place of business."

Dash did that slow head turn again and looked at me. "It's your lucky day, punk."

He turned and grabbed the woman under the arms and pulled her up, leaned her against the fender, opened the door, then grabbed her as she started to sink again and put her in the car with all the delicacy of a carny folding up a circus tent.

Turning, he studied me, raised his hand and made a finger gun of it, and brought his thumb down slowly, said, "Pow."

He got in his car, an old Dodge, started it up, and drove out of there.

That night when I got home Mom was fixing some pinto beans she had soaked, adding whatever goodness it was she added to them, and she was heating up some collard greens in a pan next to them. The greens were what was left from the night before, and she had made two pans of cornbread. One had jalapeños in it like I liked, and the other didn't, like Dad liked. They had been pulled from the oven and were on the wooden block on the drain board, ready to be sliced and lined with butter.

"You all right?" she said. "Look like you walked over your grave."

"I'm fine," I said.

"Well, okay. You sure?"

"Yeah. I'm fine."

"All right then, supper'll be ready before long."

I went into the bathroom and took a shower, combed my hair in front of the mirror, wrapped a towel around my waist, and went into my room.

We didn't have much in the way of money, but being an only child allowed me to have my own space. It was dark in my room. I pretty much kept the curtains drawn. There was an air conditioner in the window, and I went over and turned it on and soon the stale air in the room began to fade and turn cool. I dropped the towel and put on some underwear and went over and laid down on the bed and thought about what had happened.

I wasn't sure why I didn't tell my mother about it, but I think it was because I was a little ashamed. I hadn't stood up for that woman and she had stood up for me. But the worst of it was she had gone home with Dash, as he was called, and if he hit her like that in public, what the hell did he do in private?

Not long after that, Dad came home from work. I heard him come in, heard my mom say, "Supper's near ready," to him.

I got up and put on some jeans and a T-shirt, slipped on my socks and shoes, and went to eat.

I thought about the event for a few days, dodged going to

that station when I needed gas, went to a Conoco on the other side of town, which was no great journey, as town took about fifteen minutes to cross.

After a while, the whole thing faded from my mind, but I was in the downtown Piggly Wiggly one day, shopping for a few things for Mom, when I saw the woman from the filling station come in. She walked slowly with her head down, and through the front plate glass I could see Dash's Dodge in the parking lot, and he was outside of it, leaning on the hood, smoking a cigarette, dressed just as he had been the day I first crossed his path.

The woman moved swiftly past the checkout counter, on into the depths of the store, grabbing a buggy as she went. She was about to start shopping when she looked up and saw me. She looked like a raccoon. Both eyes were black, and the bruises were fresh. She had a knot on the side of her head that was lumped up like there was a rock under her skin. It was the first time I got a good look at her, and without the knot and the black eyes, I could see an attractive woman there, someone who had given up on being attractive. Her hair was tied back severely, as if to match her existence, and when she saw me looking at her, I knew she recognized me too.

She turned quickly with her basket and went down a row of groceries. I couldn't help myself. As my dad once said about my mom and me, if something was not our business, we'd be sure to stick our nose into it.

I tried not rush up behind her, but instead went along

the left side of the aisle, as she pushed her cart along the right side. She turned and looked as I came up on her left, said, "Now you go on."

"I just wanted to say I'm sorry he hit you because of me."

"He hits me on account of anything. But you stay out of it. It's husband and wife business."

"It's not the way my parents do it."

"It's the way Dash does it, and that's my concern. It's in the Bible."

"What is?"

"A woman obeying her husband. I smarted and got corrected."

She had stopped pushing the basket now, and we were standing in the aisle talking. She wouldn't look directly at me, kept her head turned slightly to the side.

"That may be, but you don't have to take this kind of thing. You don't have to. Call the cops on him."

"I did. Know what they said? It's husband and wife business, not our business, not law business."

"If this isn't their business, I don't know what is."

"I know this. I got a worse beating after that, and I've learned to live with it."

"You call this living?"

"Who are you to know anything. You're a kid. Let me tell you something. Enjoy being your age, and skip marrying. You do, your life is over. It's all downhill after that. Life is a misery. I got the next life to take care of me."

You can't argue with people who are that deep in religion, so I didn't. I said, "I don't know it has to be that way, but if you get tired of it being that way, why don't you leave?"

"A wife is supposed to stick with her husband through thick and thin."

"And he's supposed to be a husband, not use you for a heavy bag."

"You go on now, ain't nothing going to change. I take too long in here, he sees me talking to you, it wouldn't be good for either of us."

She abruptly shoved the basket forward and went down the aisle, pausing to pick up some cans of soup and drop them into the buggy.

I got the RC Cola I had come in for and a bag of peanuts. I paid for them and went out. I glanced at Dash. He wasn't looking at me. He was still leaning on his car, smoking a cigarette. I walked on down the sidewalk and out to the side of the Piggly Wiggly and got in my car. I opened my drink with a church key I had in the car. I drank a bit of the cola, then opened my bag of peanuts and poured them down the neck of the bottle and listened to the salty nuts fizz in the soda. When it settled, I took a swig and chewed the wet peanuts. I felt like I ought to do something about that poor woman, but I didn't know what.

I backed the car out with one hand and held my drink in the other, and then I drove home to shower and go on a date with a girl I had wanted to go out with for some time. I began to think about that. I didn't think about the woman anymore. Like before, she and her situation drifted to the back of my teenage mind as they had before and rested there silently.

Several months crawled by, and one day as I was driving up to the Piggly Wiggly to do some shopping for Mom, I saw Minnie going inside. She looked older to me than the time before, stooped, walked as if dragging a ball and chain.

Inside I caught up with her as she pushed a basket down the aisle.

She said, "You again."

"Listen. I'm not trying to meddle."

"That's exactly what you're doing."

"Sorry. Fair enough. I'll go on."

Before I had made more than a couple of steps, she said, "Thank you. If there was something I could do, I would do it."

I moved closer to her. "You can leave."

"And go where?"

"Don't you have any relatives?"

"I have a sister in Lubbock."

"Are you on good terms with her?"

"Yes. But I haven't spoken to her in several years. Dash doesn't like me talking to people. Anyone, but especially men. He's outside in the car, you know, listening to the radio."

I thought for a moment, said, "Listen, here's what I can do. I have enough in my pocket to put you on a bus and send you to your sister's, if you'll do it. I'll give you a little more so you can buy something to eat."

"That's expensive."

"Not really," I said, though I knew I would be spending my money plus the money Mom gave me to buy groceries.

She stood there for a long moment, thinking.

"You'd do that?"

"I would."

"He's watching for me to come out, you know."

"I'll pull around back. He probably doesn't even remember me or my car."

"Enough he blacked my eyes and . . . Well, it was rough."

In that moment, when she looked at me with her bottom lip fat and cracked, her face aged, her body bent, I wanted to kill that man. But what I said was, "You decide to do it. I'll drive around back and pick you up and take you to the bus station."

She nodded. "Okay. Okay. But please, don't let him see me. He stops me, he might kill me this time."

I went outside and spotted Dash sitting in his car behind the wheel, nodding to music. I couldn't hear what it was because the windows were rolled up. I was glad for that. I would have hated for it to be a favorite song of mine that I would ever after have to associate with him.

I drove my car around back and went inside there, walked through the storage area, waving at a friend of mine who had a summer job working for Coca-Cola putting out bottles of Coke.

"What's up, Hap?"

"Nothing much," I said. "Giving a friend a ride."

Inside the store she was waiting, having abandoned the buggy. I guided her through the back and past my friend, who waved again, and we went out to my car and I drove her to the bus station.

Inside I bought her a ticket and gave her some coins to call her sister. When she came back from the pay phone, she said everything was all right. That her sister wanted to help, and so on. If she hadn't wanted to help, I guess I would have been out a ticket. I gave her the rest of the money I had, and then I sat with her for about an hour until the bus arrived. I walked her out to the bus. She looked miraculously younger; her chin was lifted, her eyes had a sparkle.

As she was about to step on the bus, she said, "I'll never forget you."

"All right if you do," I said. "I hope everything is fine with your sister."

As she stepped on the lower bus step to go through the door, I said, "Good luck, Minnie."

She nodded at me and got on the bus. The door hissed closed, and I went back to my car and drove home, needing to explain to my mother that her grocery money was on its way to Lubbock.

I continued to work part-time at the police station and jail, sweeping and mopping, feeding the prisoners, who were mostly overnight visitors who couldn't stay away from the bottle. I became friendly with the chief and his officers. I can't say I felt like one of the boys, but I felt good enough.

As for the woman, Minnie, I felt good about that, and sometimes when I tucked in for the night, I thought of my good deed and felt like a comic book hero, even though all I had done was buy a bus ticket and give her some lunch money.

I even saw Dash at the station one night, roaring drunk. They had him come in and sit on a bunk in one of the cells, left him there for a while without locking the door. They had me make him coffee, which I brought to him, a bit nervous-like, but he didn't recognize me. He drank the coffee, and a little later he was less drunk, and he napped, and then he woke up and had a pulled pork sandwich they brought in for him.

Hilo came in shortly before my shift was to end. They had given me extra hours on my summer job by adding a night shift. I was working about six hours a day. Three in the morning, and three at night. During the middle of the day they had what we called a colored man back then come in and polish the cops' shoes and do more severe cleaning than I did. They called him Pop. He had a limp from when a tire he was airing up at filling station got too much air and blew and the rim hit him in the leg and crippled him a little. He always walked like his right leg was sleepy and couldn't keep up.

Hilo sat with Dash, who was groggy, but doing okay, and they laughed about how drunk he'd been, and so on. The whole thing made me uncomfortable.

Seeing Dash in the cell earlier made me think of the woman that night when I crawled into bed, and I wondered how she was doing and what kind of life she was having. I had a hard time sleeping.

It was the very next day that I saw her. After school I drove over to the Piggly Wiggly to get myself an RC and a bag of peanuts, and when I parked and got out, I saw her walking away from the store. I thought at first it was someone who just reminded me of her, but there was something about the way she held her head, how she walked, but with a worse limp than before, that had me walk and catch up with her as she passed the corner of the store. I wanted to see if it was really her, and damn if it wasn't.

When I got up next to her, she shifted me a fearful look, reminding me of a mouse that had seen a hawk's shadow. She looked terrible. Her eyes were blacked and her nose had a knot on it and her lips were busted and scabby.

"Minnie. What are you doing here?"

"You go on now."

"No. What are you doing here?"

She hadn't stopped walking, and I was walking with her.

"You don't want him to see you, now."

"You went to Lubbock. Why did you come back?"

She stopped, looked at me. "Oh, kid. You don't know nothing. He come and got me. He come and got me that very week. He knew where I went. Where else was there for me to go?"

"You didn't have to go back with him."

"Yeah. I did. It's in the Bible. I'm to obey."

"Oh, hell, Minnie. That isn't true, even if it is in the Bible. Some Old Testament bullshit."

"Don't talk like that."

I didn't normally talk like that around women and adults then, but in that moment, I sure did. I couldn't hold it in.

"Look what you've come back to. Why?"

"Didn't have no other place to go, and he come and got me and put me in the car, and I've accepted that. I smart-mouthed him and he gave me this just this morning. I've learned my lesson. His word is law, and that's how it is. That's my life."

"That's no life. You don't deserve this."

She lifted a hand in the direction of her face.

"I had it coming."

"No you didn't."

"You go on and leave me alone now. Nothing you can do for me. Nothing anyone can do for me. You go on. Don't bother me again."

I stood on my spot and watched her limp off down the

sidewalk with the attitude of an outcast leper, limp on across the park where there were seesaws and swings and tall oaks and pecan trees, and the shadows of the trees lay over her like a shroud.

PART II.

I was downstairs in the police station, sweeping up the corridor with a dust mop, when he came staggering in the front door and partially collapsed near the receptionist's desk, leaving tracks through a place I had just mopped. He kind of heaved himself forward, made as if he was about to burp, defeated the need, said, "I think I done been poisoned."

What?" Constance said. She was a middle-aged lady with a pile of dark hair on her head stacked so high she almost needed a donkey ride to reach the top of it.

Right then the man went to his knees and his wad of greasy dark Elvis hair fell on his forehead and into his eyes. He tried to get his feet under him, but they weren't interested. He let out with a groan like he was passing a turd full of razor blades, then fell on the tile.

I knew the man, and what passed through my mind was

pretty cruel. Whatever was wrong with him, it couldn't happen to bigger and more deserving asshole than that guy.

I had two weeks left on the cop shop job before I started back to school. It was my last year. I liked the money I was getting, but I was bored with the job, and to tell you the truth, the whole thing just depressed me. You can only be around drunks and crazed rednecks so long before you either go numb or you start to be like them. I wanted to finish up my senior year and get on with my life, do whatever it was I was going to do. I wanted out of Marvel Creek. You might call it a one-horse town, and if you did, that horse was crippled and blind in one eye and needed to be put down.

It was Dash, Minnie's husband. He had threatened to fight me once, but since then I had seen him a couple times in the jail, sleeping off a drunk, and he didn't seem to recognize me. Maybe it was because my hair had grown out a bit, but more likely it was because the alcohol didn't help his memory any.

Hilo came out from the back. A lean, handsome cop who always looked crisp and polished, a man I had once admired. Over time, I liked him less, if for no other reason than he was a friend of the wife-beater, good ole boy, Dash.

I put my mop aside and went over and helped Hilo lift Dash up and we stretched him out on a bench and put a book from the receptionist's desk under his head. It was a thick and ragged hardback of *Gone With the Wind*.

"Dash," Hilo said. "Can you hear me, fella?"

Dash couldn't hear him. He had grown as white as the peaks of the Himalayas except for little pink clouds that spotted his skin around the cheeks. I could hear him breathing. It didn't sound like distressed breathing, but nonetheless, it didn't take Ben Casey to tell he was in bad way. Lassie would have given up on him.

Constance called an ambulance, and since they were pretty much next door, they were there in a matter of seconds, parking outside at the curb, then coming up the walk between the pecan trees with a stretcher. I held the door open for them.

They put Dash on the stretcher and carried him out, one arm dangling, his knuckles nearly dragging the ground.

Hilo said, "I want you to go over to the hospital with him."

"Me?"

"Who the hell else am I talking to?"

"I'm not a cop."

"No, you ain't. But I'm all that's here at the station now, and you have just been promoted to cop helper. Go over there and find out what the doctors say and come back and tell me. If he's been poisoned, I want to know how. He may have just got some spoiled food, but the way he came in, I got to wonder. Now go on. Drive over there. No use getting in a hurry. They got him."

This was a fine howdy-do. I hated that bastard, and now I had to go check on him, babysit a bit. Hilo, of course, didn't know I had been in a situation with him, and I didn't tell him. I just went out the door and started walking to my car, which was parked out to the side in the parking lot next to a line of sweetgums.

The wind was stiff and hot as a mad dog's pecker. I felt heavy and tired immediately in the summer heat, as if the weather had a wool-gloved hand and was pressing down on the top of my head. I was instantly coated in sweat, and inside my car, the back of my shirt stuck to the seat covers.

I didn't get in any rush. I drove to the Dairy Queen and stopped and went inside and got myself an ice cream cone and ate it sitting in a booth, then I bought a tall paper cup of Coke with shaved ice in it and drove over to the hospital. I finished the Coke in the car and got out and made my way inside as if I were going to my own execution.

Not everything was air-conditioned back then, but the hospital was, and the cool air made the sweat on the back of my shirt feel good. I went to the registration counter, where a woman with hair that could compete with Constance's sat in a chair and smiled at me. She wouldn't tell me anything about Dash's condition, and for some reason, she was reluctant to tell me what room he was in. I told her I was sent there by the police, but if she was moved by that information, she concealed it.

I found a candy striper who was hustling through the hospital. She was a cute brunette girl and the outfit made her cuter. I knew her a little from school and would have liked to know her better. I stopped her and told her who I was looking for, stressing I worked for the police department, to see if I could impress her. Like the receptionist, if I had she held her excitement close to her chest. But she did show me where to go by walking down the hall with me. Her perfume was heavenly and prominent enough I could have closed my eyes and followed her scent.

When I was at his room, my candy striper companion headed out and left me feeling sad and wistful. The door was partially open. I looked inside. He wasn't in there, but I understood then this was the room where he would end up.

I went and sat in a chair in the hallway and watched some more candy stripers go by in their cute uniforms. They were all pretty. I recognized some of them from school but didn't really know any of them.

I sat there hoping Dash would die, and his wife Minnie would be free, and then I felt bad about it for a time, and then I decided I still wished him dead, and kept wishing, as if that really mattered. As my dad said, "Shit in one hand, wish in the other, and see which one fills up first."

After a while they wheeled Dash into the room assigned to him. I went over and spoke to the doctor when he came out of the room, told him I had been sent over by the police department, and they wanted to know how he was and what was wrong.

"I can only talk to the police or a family member. You're neither."

"Cops sent me over."

"Tell them to send someone else over. With authority."

That gave me a way out. I went back to the station, but they were still short-handed, including the chief, so Hilo told me to drive over to Dash's house and see if his wife knew that he was in the hospital, did she even know he was sick and maybe poisoned somehow. He gave me the address.

The idea that anyone would do that now, have a citizen do the cops' work for them, is unthought of. But back then, in the sixties, in small towns, they sort of made up their own rules.

I drove over there, and it was out in the country a little, down a red clay road. A car in front of me was driving fast, and the dry red dust rose up in clouds, and when I drove through the clouds, the dust coated my windshield.

I was thinking it was a good day to be home in front of the window fan, reading, or maybe out fishing with my friend Leonard. Me and him, we knew all the good fishing holes.

When I came to the house, I parked in the dirt driveway. It wasn't a good house. It was small and had last been painted about the time of the Pliocene. Gray shingles flapped on the roof like hot tongues begging for water. Where they lifted up, I could see tar paper. There was tar paper over some of the windows too, and the steps in front of the door sagged a little to one side.

I walked with hesitation up the drive, mounted the

leaning steps, and knocked on the door. No one answered. I went around back, and as I did, I had a queasy feeling if I knocked on the back door she might answer this time, and I would see her wearing her raccoon eyes and knotted forehead from his blows. Her nose might be broken, her lip fat. I didn't like the idea of that. I knocked, but no one answered back there either. There was a fan humming in the window by the door. It had a screen wire netting over the back with flies resting on it. There were always flies resting on the back of a cooler, or most anything that time of year.

I walked around front and got a little notepad and a pencil out of my car and wrote out a note and stuck it in the crack between the screen door and the door frame and drove out of there.

I hadn't gone more than a mile when I saw some crows rise up, startled by my motor. They flew off quick, having come out of a swirl of blackberry vines that grew along-side the road. Beyond the vines was a ditch, and because I was coming up on a hill I could see down into it, and there was something odd in it. At first, I thought it might be a store mannequin, what we called a dummy back then, but I recognized what the shape was wearing. The same dress Minnie always wore, thin and gray and sad-looking.

Feeling a knot growing in the pit of my stomach, I parked the car on the edge of the road, got out, and made my feet move, went over to look in the ditch.

It was indeed poor Minnie.

I gathered myself and slid down into the ditch and took a look at her. Flies were buzzing on her eyes and in her open mouth. Her face was battered and she had fat finger marks against her neck. I shooed the flies and went back to my car and got an old blanket I had in the back seat and took it down and put it over her after I shooed the flies again. Her feet stuck out under the short blanket. She had on one shoe. I found the other one nearby, and for whatever reason, I slipped it on her bare foot, which was more difficult than I would have imagined. She was pretty stiff. None of this was something you should do with a crime scene, but I didn't know that back then, and frankly, I'm not sure a lot of our police knew it, and I don't know if it would have mattered to me. I felt she should be covered and have her shoe on. Great police work was most likely unnecessary. We had our share of murders in and around Marvel Creek, but it was usually obvious who did it, and I felt this was pretty obvious as well.

When I got back in the car, my hands were trembling, and I could hardly turn the key. I wanted to go to the hospital and smother Dash in his sleep. I wanted to do a lot of things to him, and none of them good.

Finally, I got the motor humming and drove back to the station.

There was quite a bit of excitement over the next couple of days about Minnie's murder and Dash being in the hospital. It was a real-life murder mystery, the paper said, but it didn't seem that mysterious to me. I had gotten Minnie away from that horrid bastard once, and then she had gone back to him, and now this.

I gave my statement to Hilo, and then a reporter came around to see me, but I didn't tell him much. I had him talk to Hilo.

Next day I heard them chatting around the station. Dash had indeed been poisoned. Arsenic was suspected, rat poison the culprit. Found on the stove at Dash's house was a large pot of minestrone soup, and at the bottom of the pot two rats, dead of poison it was surmised.

No doubt about it, Minnie had boiled a couple of poisoned rats in his soup, hoping to put him down. It was suspected that she had liberally dosed the soup with rat poison too.

Hilo had been to the hospital to talk to Dash a couple of times, and he said Dash grinned and said, "I thought it was some of the best soup she had ever made. The rats gave it flavor for once."

As for Minnie, well, a woman who picked up soda bottles to sell came into the station the day after I found the body, and said, "I seen that woman that got killed. Seen her picture in the paper. One that boiled the poisoned rats in that man's soup."

I was mopping the lower floor bathroom, the one the receptionist and the cops used, when that woman came in, but I could hear her talking clearly. She sat in a chair at the receptionist's desk, and Hilo pulled a chair up for himself, and Constance wrote down what the woman said in shorthand to be typed up later.

"I like to pick up pop bottles. I carry me a bag, and if I have a good day, I can darn near fill it. I fill it, well, then I can't carry it. I walk that road once a week to get them tossed bottles, but I won't no more, not since they found that woman dead, and then of course, there's the colored man."

"Who would that be?" Hilo said.

"I seen him that very day. He was walking along the railroad tracks. It was that fella that sharpens lawn mower blades and such."

"You mean Calabash?"

"That's him. Yeah. I seen him walking along the tracks, and then when I heard they found that dead woman, well I put two and two together and come here to give you my arithmetic."

I backed out of the bathroom, still mopping, listening.

"You see, it was along about the same time the paper said she must have been killed. I figured that big buck got her."

"That makes some things clear," Hilo said.

I thought: what's clear is Dash killed her.

I went mopping along the hall, and pretty soon I was at the end of it and couldn't hear them anymore.

About a half hour later, I couldn't stand it, so I found Hilo. He was in his small office with a rotating fan on a table next to him. He was rocked back in his chair with his feet on his desk, drinking a bottle of grape soda.

He looked up as I came in, almost smiled.

"Hey, boy. Take a load off."

I sat down in the chair in front of his desk. The fan rotated my way and cooled me for an instant before turning back toward Hilo and leaving me in the heat.

I said, "Hilo, I know you know Dash beat his wife."

"Now and again."

"He hurt her pretty bad and she reported here but wasn't nothing done about it."

Hilo's face soured. "Listen here. We know Dash and his wife fought. Husbands and wives do that."

"I'm not talking about having an argument."

"Some women, they just don't know when to shut up. Dash had to pop her one now and again. It was for her own good."

"Her own good? How is her being dead in a ditch for her own good?"

"Whoa now. Dash is a good ole boy. He didn't kill her. Fact is, pretty sure we know who done it. You know the big nigger works here shining shoes and such, takes your place in the summer."

"Pop? He gets around so slow Minnie would have had to strangle herself. Besides, he doesn't sharpen lawn mower blades."

"I mean Pop's son. He was the one she seen near the railroad tracks, not far from the ditch where you found Minnie."

"That don't mean he did it."

"It means he likely did it. He's been in prison for rape and was suspected in a murder once. His own cousin. She had gone off with him and was found in the river bottoms next day, naked with her throat cut. He's had a bit of trouble around town more than once after that. Had light fingers. He seems likely for it."

"But Dash beat his wife regularly. Gave her a limp. She reported it to the station here. No one did anything."

"She could have left at any time. Staying was her choice. Again, boy. Husband and wife business."

"Sounds to me like murder is Dash's business."

Hilo's face colored, and he pulled his feet off his desk and settled into place and slammed the bottle of grape soda down on his desk hard enough to make me jump a little. Little beads of the drink bounced in the air and splashed on the back of his hand and onto the desk.

"You ain't no goddamn policeman, boy. I've known Dash all my life. We hunt and fish together. He's a good ole boy. His wife, she was a real bitch. She had ideas about how she should do this or that, and he didn't want her to. Man has the say, not the wife. She had to be corrected now and then for smartin' off or trying to wear the pants in the family."

"Did that correction and those pants get her in that ditch?"

"You talking pretty sharp to a man you work for. You got about a week and a half to go. You don't have to finish out."

I thought of the gas I wanted to put in my car, and I shut my mouth. I'm not proud of that. All I can tell you is I was seventeen.

The storm cloud on Hilo's face went away, and he grinned. "It's all right. You're just saying your piece. But now you've said it. Go on back to work, now. We won't talk about it no more. It's best we don't, hear?"

I nodded and went out, ashamed of myself for agreeing.

I was coming back from the café after lunch, when I saw a struggle out front of the station. There were three cops, Hilo one of them, grappling with a big black man, trying to get him up the steps. He was throwing them loose of him like a dog shedding water.

He knocked one of the cops out in the yard and up against one of the pecan trees. The thrown cop got up like he didn't really want to and went back at it. Finally, one of the cops dove for his legs and Calabash fell and his head cracked on the steps, and it was a loud crack, like a car tire rolling over a walnut. They eventually got him up and into the station, and I came in as they were trying to wrestle him upstairs to the jail cells.

It was quite the fight. Smacking his head on that step outside hadn't worried him long. Hilo came rolling down the stairs, tumbling out on the lower floor. When he went back up, his face red with embarrassment, he pulled his slapjack from his belt and went to work on the big man while the other cops held him.

It was a horrible beating. Blood was on the stairs and on the walls along the stairs, and some of the blood had flown down and spotted my face where I stood in the lobby. The big man was still standing, and though he stood for a long time, even he could only take so much. He went to his knees and Hilo hit him a few more times with the slapjack, each blow hard enough to drive a nail.

They got him upstairs, and I watched them disappear around the edge of the stairway and the wall.

I don't know exactly why, but I followed them up, and when I got up there they were still working on him. Now they were punching and kicking him, and Hilo was using that slapjack like he was swatting flies, only what that poor man was getting was a lot worse than what he'd have gotten from a fly swatter.

They got him in a cell, threw him in there, and closed the door and poked a key in the lock and penned him up. The prisoner got up and stumbled to the bars and took hold of them and tried to shake them, but they were so imbedded in concrete King Kong couldn't have made them move. He did that for a moment, blood running down his face and all over his once-white shirt. His teeth were gritted in a fence of anger and were stained with blood. He sat down suddenly on the floor. His legs had turned to rubber, and once he sat, he wavered there a moment, then fell back on the cement, turned over as if to crawl, and then he was still as stone.

"Hope that nigger dies," Hilo said.

Hilo, who was always crisp and neat, looked like a long-haired cat that had been groomed with a machete. His hat was gone, his hair was sticking up like weeds in a briar patch, and his shirt was torn as well as one of his pants pockets. There was blood on his face and on his shoes. He looked in better shape than the other two.

Then he saw me. "What the fuck you looking at, boy? Get a mop. Clean this place up."

I almost threw in the towel, right then, but I had a little more than a week left, and then I was back in school. Still, I didn't move. I stood my ground and the cops passed me and went down the stairs, fuming and cussing.

I went over to the cell and looked in. The big man had woken up. He put his hands under him and made a sound a little like a dying mouse, and then slowly, as if he were building himself into place, bone by bone, muscle by muscle, he made it to his feet. He saw me looking at him.

"Go on, kid. Get the hell away from me."

I went and got the mop out of the closet, and the mop

bucket, and filled it with water and floor soap, and went to work mopping up blood on the second floor and on the stairs. Blood sheds easier than it cleans, but I got it mopped up and the walls wiped.

When I had that done, I went downstairs and told Constance that she ought to call a doctor, because the man upstairs was in a bad way.

She got up and went into the chief's office. I didn't even know he was around. He had been out for a week or so. He came out of his office with his thumbs hooked in his gun belt. He was Hilo's cousin. He was about ten years older and he was a little fat and worn-out looking.

"Is that what all that ruckus was about? A nigger whipping?"

I didn't say anything, but he could tell from my face that that was what it was about. He hadn't even bothered to come out of his office with all that fighting going on, perhaps for fear of having to deal with the big man himself.

"I was trying to do some goddamn paper work. Hilo!"

Hilo came out of the downstairs bathroom wiping his face with a bloody towel.

"What the hell happened to you? Look like you got caught up in a lawn mower."

"Nigger trouble. Jake and Earl, they're patching each other up in the back."

"He whipped all three of you?"

"He's the one in the cell."

"But it took all three of you?"

"I hadn't never had hold of anyone like that. It was like fighting a goddamn octopus."

"He the one that lady, whatever her name is, reported?"

"Yes, sir."

"I assume you asked him if he'd come in before you decided to flail on him?"

"Yes, sir. He didn't have a mind to come in. Said he didn't do nothing."

"Might not have."

"Well, sir. He's got a record."

"Investigate it. Maybe give him a solid interrogation, if you know what I mean. But I think you're going to need more men and maybe a hammer."

Hilo didn't like that he hadn't been able to handle the man upstairs better than he had. And, of course, now I knew they were talking about Calabash, the one they decided had strangled poor Minnie.

Pop's hands were like leather mitts and his face looked to have been irrigated, his wrinkles were so deep. His hair was snow white and cut close, and his eyes were as sad as those paintings of Jesus on the cross, and they had scar tissue above them, thick as tree bark and similar in appearance. He was big and slightly bent, and when he walked, he lumbered and limped. When I saw him, he was usually carrying his shoe box. He worked at the barbershop now and then shining shoes and was brought into the police station to do the same for the cops from time to time, and when the summer was gone, he would be my replacement at the jail and police station as janitor and errand runner. There was a rumor that he had once been a professional boxer.

He came into the station without his shoe box and asked politely at the front desk if he could see his son, and got the nod. He went upstairs behind me. I was carrying my mop bucket up to do some work in the back room, and frankly, when I realized he was going up, I started ahead of him, being curious.

I went on into the janitor closet just beyond the cells, near the room where they interrogated people, sometimes with words, sometimes with fists. I slowly went about pouring dirty water out of the bucket down the drain and refilling it with fresh hot water from the floor sink.

I got the bucket full, added a bit of floor soap, and put a new mop head on the mop. Pop had arrived and pulled up a folding chair that had been against the wall and parked it in front of the cell and eased himself into it. I could see him through the crack in the door as I went about my preparations.

"What you done got yourself into, boy?"

"I didn't do nothing," Calabash said.

"You've done something before."

"Said I didn't do nothing. Before ain't now."

"You always doing something."

"Back then, yeah, not now. How come you don't never stand up for me?"

"You got to stand up first."

"Self-righteous, ain't you, old man? You always got the do-right talk, but you ain't nothing but an old Uncle Tom. They snipped your nuts long ago."

"You weren't behind them bars, I'd slap your face, boy."

"Tell them to let you in."

"You ain't the bad man you think."

"Tell that to all them cops it took to put me in here. Tell them that. You fought some in the day, but you ain't nothing now. Not a thing. I could bend you over my knee and paddle your ass way you used to do me."

"You're not tough. Not in the way it counts. You're just mean and low down. I never could understand you."

"No. You never could."

I had the rolling bucket ready now, so I pushed it out of the closet with the mop and gently closed the door. Pop looked up when I did. It was like he had just noticed I was upstairs.

Pushing the bucket along, I made my way to the back room. I could still hear them talking.

"You done this, you ought to come clean, boy. You done this, you got to pay."

"Ever nigger ever born pays, old man. Even the Uncle Toms. Where's being the good nigger got you, huh?"

"You don't need to use that word about our people. Let the white man use it, not you."

"We let them do it a lot."

"Our day will come."

"You still counting on Moses to bring you to the promise land, old man?"

"I'm counting on time."

"Not in your time, old man. You got maybe a year or two left, and you'll be leaning on the door to hell."

"That's your place to go," said Pop.

"You want me to tell them I did it so I can fry like ham in the electric chair? That what you want?"

"It's your soul I'm worried about."

"I ain't got no soul."

"I hate to hear that, son. I really do."

"You ain't got one neither. Ain't no one got none. Us niggers ain't even got a toilet in town. Got to piss out behind a building, and heaven help you if anyone sees you do it. Then you're showing your stuff. Can't buy a goddamn hamburger without going through the back door. I'd like a place to eat and I'd like a place to shit in town, same as white folks. Look over there at that commode. I ought to rip it out of the wall, lean up against the bars, and shit through it. Mess on the floor there."

"You just being vulgar. Ought to be a man, Calabash. That's what you ought to be. Your mama—"

"Don't bring her into this. She done worked herself to death. She worked herself to death for Jesus and Heaven tomorrow. When it come tomorrow, she just died, old man. Just died."

"You don't know a thing about her. She raised you, and you don't know a thing about her."

"Go on now. I'm through with you, Uncle Tom. I'm ashamed to say you my daddy. All you did was shoot some juice in a good woman. You ain't no kind of daddy."

"Don't talk like that."

You just say what's supposed to be right, and ain't none of it right. Come up here close, old man. I got something to tell you. You want to hear something, I got it for you."

I heard Pop's chair scrape closer, and they said something else to each other, something soft. I swished my mop past the open door, and Pop was close to the bars looking in at Calabash. I could just see Calabash's face. He had it pressed tight against the bars and he was saying something to Pop, something mean. I saw Pop sink in his shoes, and then he started shuffling toward the stairs.

"Put that in your pipe and smoke it," Calabash said as Pop moved away.

Pop looked at me as I swished back across the doorway. He smiled a little. It was a habit smile, not a real one. It reminded me of one I had seen him give the cops in the station, right after they insulted him: a hard, little smile full of pain and remembrance.

Nodding, he went on down the stairs and I went back to mopping.

"Hey, white boy," Calabash called out to me.

I left the mop in the bucket and went over to where Pop had left the chair.

"Hey, boy. Why don't you drop your pants and back up to the bars here and I'll fuck you. You'd like a black snake, wouldn't you?"

I didn't say anything. I took the chair from where Pop left it and put it against the wall and went back to mopping. I could hear Calabash laugh and then he was quiet, and then I thought I heard a noise like someone with a cold, and then he was quiet again.

Later, when I put the mop up, I glanced in the cell. Calabash was lying on his cot with his arm flung over his eyes.

It wasn't none of my business, so I got right on it.

I went over to the hospital to see Dash, but he wasn't in. They had let him go home, though I was assured he was doing poorly. I think the nurse who told me this thought I was on a police matter, a helper they had sent for information, and I let her believe it. No one had before, or no one thought it mattered, so it was all right to have a moment of power, minor as it might have been.

Driving over to Dash's house, I was trying to figure how I would go about what I had in mind, but nothing presented itself, so I just drove there and got out and knocked on the door.

After a long time, the door opened, and there was Dash. The poison had given him a stroke. He limped along on his left leg, his left fist clenched.

When he saw me at the door, I could tell he didn't recognize me. He never did. Right then, though, hating him as much as I did, seeing gray in his hair he hadn't had before, him weak and pale like that, I felt sorry for him. I'm always like that. So is my mother. My father is kind, but he isn't sentimental about assholes. I sometimes think I'm sentimental about everything and everybody.

"Who are you?"

"I work at the police department. You've seen me there."

"Yeah. Long-haired kid. What do you want?"

"Calabash. I don't think he killed your wife. I'm thinking it was you."

For a moment his pale face had some color.

"Who the fuck did you say you are? You're not old enough to be a cop. Shit, boy. I didn't kill anybody, but I could start with you."

"I think if the next line is 'I'm going to get my gun,' you should note that I got you beat if it comes to a foot race."

"You think you're a funny little fucker, don't you?"

"I think there's an innocent man about to be railroaded for murdering your wife, and you did it."

"She damn sure deserved it, but it wasn't me. It was that nigger. Calabash. He did it. Get the hell out of here. I don't want you around. Why'd you come here?"

"Just wanted you to know someone knows, even if there may not be a damn thing I can do about it."

"You don't know your ass from a hole in the ground."

"I'm the one who put her on a bus so she could see her sister. But you went and got her."

"That was you . . . Oh hell. I know you. I not only seen you at the jail, you was the one at the filling station. See that now, you long-haired motherfucker. I should have kicked your ass."

"Should have tried, but instead you took it out on a woman that might have weighed a hundred and twenty pounds with rocks in her pocket. She wanted to be away from you, but you made her stick. You treated her like she was a cow you bought at an auction."

A crooked smile crawled across his face.

"Not quite. You can fuck a cow, but you can't get them to do laundry. Besides, I went to her sister's, and she was ready to come home. She didn't have no money, except what little I gave her."

"It had to be very little."

"You need to go on and get out of my business. I'm going to phone Hilo and tell him about you. You won't have that job long."

"Go ahead. I just wanted you to know I know, and I think the law and such know, but it's easier to pick on some black man who can take the fall for you. Hitting a woman like that. Shit, you ought to have poisoned yourself and been glad to do it."

"Go on, kid. I've had enough of you. I was at myself I'd whip your ass all over the yard. Shit, boy. What you think? They're going to arrest me on some suspicion you got? Them boys know me. Hilo especially. Women, you got to keep them dick-whipped. Man's woman is a man's woman, and she has to know her place. The Bible says that."

"That's one reason I gave up religion. As for her place, I think she sure showed you yours. How were those poisoned mice in minestrone?"

"Get off my place."

"Gladly."

I hadn't really accomplished anything, but I wanted that mean, poisoned, crippled son of a bitch to know someone knew, and Minnie mattered to someone, even if I only knew her from a few short conversations.

Dash went back inside, maybe to get his gun, and I went out to the car, walking pretty fast, just in case he had that gun close and handy.

I didn't have any doubt my sweeping and mopping days at the jail were done, and probably before I could get back there. Dash would be on the phone already.

I didn't give a shit. I had had it up to the top of my head with all the crap that went on down there, all the crap I was learning that went on underneath the façade of my little Andy of Mayberry town.

Driving up to park in front of the station, next to the curb near the great pecan tree, I saw Pop limping up the steps and going inside. He had his shine box with him. They had probably called him over to shine cop shoes, which struck me as brutal, considering his son was in a cell upstairs. The back of Pop's shirt had a V of sweat on it and it was stuck to him. The sides of the steps had a concrete support, and he had the box in one hand and the other on the support, using it to help him move up the steps. All in all, he was moving swiftly.

I got out of my car and saw a squirrel at the base of the pecan. He gave me a cautious look, then jetted up the trunk and into the green leaves above.

The air was still and smelled like an oncoming rain.

When I was inside, I saw Pop turn up the stairs. I decided before they fired me, I would go up and tell Pop goodbye. I stopped and let him reach the top before I started up. When I got to the top of the stairs, Hilo was there, coming out of the back room. He had his hat in his hand and his hair was ruffled from having been cooling himself off in front of the window fan.

"I got a call, boy."

"I know," I said.

"You might as well pack up anything you got up here and take it with you."

"You don't get to fire me," I said. "I quit."

"Think of it any way you like. Chief done told me you're through here, now, next year, anytime."

"Glad of it."

"Don't get smart with me."

"I'm not getting smart, I'm getting my work shoes, and then I'm saying bye to Pop, and I'm gone."

That's when I noticed Hilo wasn't looking at me anymore. He was looking down the gap that led to the cells. His brow was wrinkled. He dropped his hat.

I turned and looked down there too.

Pop had a pistol. It was a big revolver and looked old enough to have been used in the Civil War. He cocked the hammer back and pointed it at the cell where his son was.

I glanced back at Hilo. He was drawing his gun. He had it halfway out of his holster when his left eye and half his face jumped away from him and slapped against the wall with a sound like a wet rag. The wall smeared red.

I turned and looked at Pop. The gun was pointed in my direction. He studied me for a long moment. He turned back to the cell.

"You ain't never gonna do right," he said, and cocked back that single-action again.

I took one step forward without even realizing it. I should have gone down those stairs like a hurricane, but I took that one step for whatever reason, and when I did, I could see Calabash standing in his cell, his hands on the bars.

"That's right. What you can't fix you shit on," Calabash said.

"You sure can't be fixed," Pop said.

"Go ahead. Do me a goddamn favor."

The gun snapped and nothing happened. The load was

bad. Pop cocked back the hammer again, causing the cylinder to rotate.

"It's best, son."

"For who?" Calabash said, and lost his nerve, backed away from the bars. The gun fired. I heard a sound like someone coughing, and then Pop cocked the gun again, and it jumped in his hand once more. Then he walked over to the cell, stuck the gun through the bars and popped off another shot. Way he was standing I couldn't still see in the cell.

I put my back to the wall as he turned and looked at me.

"Wasn't nothing for it," Pop said. "Told me he killed and raped that girl, just like last time. Said he liked it. I turned out his light, boy. I turned it out."

He dropped the pistol and walked past me, then turned and went back and got his shine box, like he had an appointment to polish shoes. He passed me again with his box, his old face suddenly smooth as a baby's ass, and went around the side of the wall and started down the stairs. I realized I had been holding my breath. I moved away from the wall and went over and looked in the cell. The back wall and floor were red with blood and Calabash was on his side. He had big red blooms of blood on his chest and abdomen. His eyes and mouth were open. He looked like a man who had found a snake in his mailbox.

I hurried back to the stairway, eased my head around the corner, saw Pop going out the front door with his box. I turned and looked at the wall. Part of Hilo's face was stuck there, but it was sliding ever so slowly down the wall, like a slug on a windowpane.

When I got downstairs, the chief was standing in front of the reception desk. He had a pistol in his hand. He looked and saw me and the pistol pointed at me. If he had looked any more frightened, there would have to have been two of him.

"Pop shot Calabash," I said. "And Hilo."

"They alive?"

"Not likely."

"I guess I better go get him." But the chief didn't move.

At home that night I would have thought I wouldn't have had an appetite, but it was as if I was a hollow in the earth that couldn't be filled.

I told my parents what had happened, and my mother tried to talk to me, but my dad said, "Let him be."

I sat at the table like always, and Mom brought out what she called Mexican Mess, and put it on my plate, and cut me some jalapeños and grated some cheese on top of it, and then brought out Mexican cornbread and butter, and all manner of other things. When we had the food, she always cooked like she was expecting the Mormon Tabernacle Choir.

She kept looking at me like she expected me to levitate or something.

Dad glanced at me now and again, but he didn't try to hold my gaze. I must have had that thing they call the thousand-yard stare. He leaned out from his chair and touched me on the shoulder gentle as a butterfly, then turned to the food Mom was heaping on his plate.

I ate more than Dad did. I ate more than anyone did since the creation of the world, and Mom even made me oatmeal on the stove after that, as I kept saying how hungry I was. By bedtime I was sick to my stomach, and ended up throwing up, and if I ate more than anyone since the creation of the world, since humans walked the earth, I also puked more than anyone ever. I thought my insides were coming out. But when it was all over, I felt marginally better, dissolved some baking soda in a glass of water, drank that to settle my stomach, and went to bed.

My life was a staggering blank for a few days, and I saw things different from then on. Colors changed, then wind blew strange, and the rain was the heavens' tears. People's voices sounded piped in from afar, and when I spoke my own voice sounded strange to me, and when I looked at people I saw flesh bags full of blood and bone, all of them heading for a ride in the hearse, a hole in the ground. My own face in the mirror was strange and pale, and my eyes were small holes that I kept staring at, trying to rediscover myself inside of them.

For a long time, I slept poorly, with the closet light on, the door to the closet partially open to spread the light across my room. Most nights I dreamed I was in the cell and Pop was pointing the revolver at me. I would then see Hilo's face on the wall, oozing down in what looked like strawberry jam spotted with bone and a clinging eyeball. I saw Calabash on his side, his eyes open, and one night, in a dream, Calabash winked at me, said, "Do me a goddamn favor."

It seemed so real I jumped awake with a yell.

Dad came in the room then. He sat in a chair by the bed. I noticed in the thin moonlight from the window that he looked tired and old for the first time in my memory. Maybe I just hadn't been paying attention. Wrinkles covered his face like map lines, and his missing teeth on one side had caused his jaw to sink. He had pulled them out when they were bad by tying a cord to a doorknob, then the other end to the tooth, and then he would slam the door by kicking it with his foot. It was cheap dentistry.

I was already sitting up when he came in. I was sweating cold sweat.

I didn't say anything to him. He sat silent for a long time, but it felt fine to have him near. I had once seen him bend a crowbar across his chest, crush an apple in his hand as if he were wadding up cellophane. If there were haints, they would fear him, not the other way around.

It startled me when he spoke.

"Thing like that, it don't never go away completely, but you learn to get on with things."

I didn't ask him how he knew what I was dreaming about. He just knew. I'm sure it wasn't the first time I had yelled in my sleep since it happened, though it was the first time it had brought me awake in the manner it had that night, and it was the first time it had brought Dad into the room, that I was aware of anyway. It was like all those nights and all those dreams had been building up to this explosive moment: the Vesuvius of nightmares.

"I thought Dash did it," I said. "I was sure he killed her."

"Another day, he might have."

My dad always thought a black man was prone to that kind of thing, murder and rape, but tonight he didn't say that. He held that back. I think he didn't want to start a fight. Not that night.

"A fella can see something like what you saw, and it can hang in the back of his mind like a goddamn bat, but finally that bat will fly off. Sometimes it'll come back and nest, but it won't be around as much as it's around now."

"How do you know?"

"Things happen in life, you live long enough," he said.

And in that instant I knew he too had seen some bad things. I didn't ask him what. I didn't want to know right then. Maybe later. But I realized, with some kind of odd comfort, that we were now, father and son, part of some rare and not-so-coveted club.

He got up and went out and came back with a damp washrag, gave it to me. "Wipe your face down, son."

I did that. He took the rag.

"Here's a thing I'm going to tell you that's all I know about a thing like this. You move on. You got to. You don't, well, that bat never flies out of the cave, just hangs around inside of it. Things that can't be changed won't be changed. You want some milk to help you sleep?"

"Okay," I said.

Dad went into the kitchen, and I heard him pouring milk into a pan, and I knew the next move would be to heat the milk on the stove.

After a bit he came in carrying a glass of warm milk with a pot holder. He sat the glass on the nightstand and left the pot holder with it.

"Don't burn yourself."

"Thanks, Dad."

"You better?"

"Yes, sir."

He gave a bit of a grunt and went out.

I drank the milk, and when I went back to bed, I thought of my dad in the next room with Mom. I thought of the sad club we belonged to, and for some reason, knowing that, I slept much better, and as the days passed, better yet. As Dad predicted, the bat flew away more often, but now and again, in an unsuspecting moment, asleep or awake, it flapped back into the little dark cave inside my head and made its presence known.

After the shooting Pop had walked down to the café and gone through the front door like a white man and found a table and sat there and placed his gun on the chair beside him. He called out for a hamburger and fries and Coke, and you can bet he got those. He sat there looking around, taking in the café, a place he had never been allowed to enter, and when the food came he started eating. One of the black cooks slipped out the back and went and fetched the police.

The chief finally arranged for some cops to get there, and they came and it was easy. Pop went without incident, giving up his gun. He only asked to finish eating the hamburger, and they let him. He went away with them then, pleaded guilty, ending up going to prison, and then the electric chair. My uncle knew a fellow worked at the Huntsville prison outside of Houston, and that fellow told him Pop had a cheeseburger, fries, and a chocolate shake for his last meal, and ate every bite. He carried a Bible with him to the execution chamber and a reverend walked at his side praying.

"The reverend walked with him," my uncle said. "He thinks niggers got their own heaven, that's what my friend told me. I ain't so sure about that. My friend, they call him Captain, said Pop looked happy to go, like he was starting out on vacation. He had his head shaved, and Captain said it was so shiny in the lights it made you have to look away, but Pop didn't have his head hung. He kept it up. Captain said he didn't have that wild dog look in his eyes they get, and when they put the cap on him he smiled and asked if it would take long.

"'Naw,' said Captain, 'but you might jump a little.' But he didn't. They hit him the first time and he was gone quick, his skull smoking under his metal hat, but by the time they gave him the backup jolt, he had done crossed Jordan in a motorboat."

They buried Calabash in a colored graveyard out in the country, and I don't know who or if anyone came to the cemetery to see him go down. I only know he got buried. I don't know where Pop ended up, but my guess is the prison graveyard, most likely unmarked.

Dash, he got better and was still alive last time I heard. I really don't want to know any more about him. Not now, not ever.

THE WATERING SHED

WHEN ME AND LEONARD were young men, we decided to drive out to the Watering Shed to drink. We were underage, but we heard Shank figured if you could drive and had money, you could drink. I didn't even drink, but the Watering Shed was a kind of rite of passage, and we wanted to go there just to prove our balls had dropped. It would be our first visit.

Leonard, being black, wasn't exactly welcome. Though on the books East Texas was integrated, a lot of white folks were having a problem embracing it.

I think Leonard half-hoped he'd be denied, and that he could cause some trouble over it. Leonard has always been kind of angry, and he may have been even more angry then.

There was also this: he was queer as a six-toed cat and

proud of it, and was as tough as a nickel steak and so masculine he made the macho tough guys look like they wore lace panties and shaved their balls.

The Watering Shed was well out in the woods, down by the river, and there were stories about how people went out there and didn't come back, were later found in the river. Shank was known to settle some matters with a baseball bat or a cutoff shotgun he kept behind the bar. As for the clientele, well, let's just say they weren't sophisticated.

Frankly, I don't know how it happened, but since Leonard and I met, we had become friends, and had bonded because of certain incidents, and truth was, we were moving beyond mere friendship and were becoming like brothers. Him being black and me being white broke some unwritten rules, and me hanging with him and him being queer, that just made it all the worse as far as many Southern folk were concerned.

When we got to the Watering Shed, there were a few cars parked out front, and the night was settling down on the world, and there was a glint of silver moonlight on the tin roof. We went in, Leonard bold as a cold, bare titty at a strip show, and me a little nervous, like a long-tailed cat in a room full of rocking chairs.

When we entered, you could have heard a microbe drop.

There was tobacco smoke in the air, and it was a little warm, and it smelled funny, an accumulation of sweat and alcohol. It wasn't packed inside, just a few folks here and there. Near the door was a round table, and there were four men at the table playing cards and drinking beer.

At the bar were two others, and in the back, at two different tables, a couple of men sat sipping beer. Joe Shank, who I knew from around town, was behind the bar. There wasn't a woman in the place.

It wasn't me they were looking at, of course, it was Leonard, black as an eggplant, cocky as a rooster. He sauntered over to the bar like Wild Bill Hickok, leaned on it, said, "Bartender, how about a beer?"

"How about some money?" Shank said.

Shank was a big redheaded guy with a big belly, but he gave you the immediate impression of someone who would charge a rhino, thinking he was going to run into its mouth and come out its ass.

Leonard paid for the beer, and Shank placed a bottle of Jax in front of him and used a church key to pop the top.

I ended up sitting on a stool next to where Leonard was standing. There was a large, flyspecked mirror behind the bar, and the bottom of it was covered by the tops of liquor bottles. I could see the men at the table by the door in it, and it was easy to turn my head and see those who were at the end of the bar and in the back. They seemed to have gone into comas, but the ones at the table by the door, they looked alert, like hungry lions that had just noticed a gazelle had wandered into their path.

"You want a beer, Hap?" Leonard said.

"No," I said.

"You might ought to have one," the bartender said.

"That's all right," I said.

"No," said the bartender, "you might ought to have one. You're taking up a drinker's space."

"You got ghosts for drinkers?" Leonard said, taking the beer Shank had set in front of him, tossing back a deep swig. "It's not like the house is full and there's a line at the door."

Shank made a grin so thin you couldn't have slipped a razor blade between his lips.

"Come into this bar, you buy a drink. You can pour it in your boot or take it in the shitter and pour it down the drain, you want, but you buy one. That, or some other liquor. What will it be?"

"A beer," I said.

"Don't want it, don't have to buy it," Leonard said.

"Yes, he does," said Shank. "He has to buy it."

"It's all right," I said.

"Not if you don't want it," Leonard said.

"Want it or don't, he's got to buy one," Shank said.

"He's gonna buy a beer," said a man at the table. I glanced at him. He was the only man at the table below thirty, probably not a whole lot older than us. He had a long face and fat lips and a lean body made hard by work, and a gleam in his eye like a man looking for a slight.

"You buying?" Leonard said, looking over his shoulder at the man at the table.

"What's that?" said the young man, turning his head slightly, like maybe if he did, Leonard's color might change.

"You heard me."

"Don't think I did."

"Ought to get your ears checked then," Leonard said. "Get them flushed out or some such, 'cause I know I'm talking clearly. You heard me, didn't you, Hap?"

"I heard you."

Shank said, "That's enough. Kid, buy a beer or hit the road."

"Sure," I said. "Jax. Whatever."

The two men at the far end of the bar picked up their beers and drifted toward the back, to a free table.

Shank went to a cooler and brought me back a bottle of Jax and set it in front of me and used the church key to pop the top off. The beer hissed a little and foamed over the rim, and I could smell the alcohol from it, a smell I've never liked.

"Enjoy," Shank said.

I looked in the mirror, at the young man at the table. He was staring at us, and not because he was trying to figure our dress size. I let the beer stay where it was, forming a wet ring on the bar, and carefully watched him in the mirror.

Leonard had turned around so he could lean his back into the bar, and he was looking at the young man and smiling between sips. He has a great smile, like a shark.

The young man said, "Shank, I think you've done let this establishment go to the fucking buzzards."

Shank said, "That's enough, Philip. That's plenty. Times change. I get paid whoever buys a beer. A turkey comes in here, wants a beer, I'll sell it to him he's wearing pants and he's got money."

"Turkey came in here, he might get plucked," Philip said.

"Only in that I jack up the prices," Shank said.

"Ain't that the truth," Leonard said. "I could have had a beer and barbecue sandwich for the price you ask."

"Then you need to go somewhere where they got a barbecue sandwich," Shank said.

"But I'd miss the company here."

"Yeah, well, it might not be as good as you think."

"Naw," Leonard said. "It's fine here. Right, Hap?"

I didn't answer. I eyed the front door without being too obvious about it. I wondered if we could make it if things got out of hand.

"I don't like your kind of business, Shank," Philip said.

"That's all right," Shank said. "You don't have to like it."

One of the men at the table gently scooted his chair back, creating a bit of distance between him and the conversation.

"Bottoms up," Leonard said, and drank the rest of the beer with a series of gulps. He put the bottle on the bar, said, "How about another one?"

"You pay, you drink," Shank said, and went to get

another Jax. He came back with it, placed it in front of Leonard, opened it with the church key, nabbed the empty, and carried it away.

"There was a time when a nigger knew his place," Philip said.

"All right, now, goddamn it," Shank said, tossing the bottle into a big can behind the bar. "I told you enough is enough. You need to hit the road, Philip, and now. Don't let your shirttail catch in the door when it closes."

Philip turned red as a new rose.

"I can't believe you'd talk to me like that," Philip said. "I come in here all the time and spend good money, and this nigger and his nigger-loving friend come in, and now you're on their side."

"I'm on my side," Shank said. "I'm running a business."

I glanced at Leonard. He was sipping his fresh beer, and didn't seem to have a care in the world. It was like he might be gathering up thoughts for future plans that evening, though I was beginning to feel any plans we might want to make were about to be cut short.

It was then that I noticed he had slipped his free hand into his pocket, and I could see something in his hand as he pulled it out. My guess was it was a pocketknife. I knew he had it set so he could thumb the blade open. It wasn't long but it was sharp. He used it to clean fish and squirrels, and I had seen him at work with it. He was as smooth as a surgeon operating on his own child.

I looked at Philip. I could see something behind his

black eyes, dark and mysterious, dangerous and bold. The air was thick with tension.

"Maybe we should go," I said.

"Sounds like a good idea," Philip said.

"No, I don't want to go, not if I'm made to go," Leonard said. "I want to leave on my own."

"Don't cause trouble, you can stay," Shank said.

That surprised me somehow. I thought Shank would tell us to leave, as we didn't exactly fit in out there, but I realized then that the macho code was at work. Shank wasn't going to be told what to do any more than Leonard was. He wasn't going to be pushed around by some customer, even if he'd just as soon me and Leonard had stayed home. Leonard, especially.

"I don't like the way things are going out here," Philip said to Shank. "I don't know I want to give you my business."

"I don't need your goddamn business," Shank said.

"I don't need this shit hole either," Philip said.

"Yeah, but it's my shit hole, and you can get your ass out and don't come back."

Philip stood up. He was wearing a loose, blue shirt with the tails hanging out, and his hand pushed his shirt up in the back.

"I can't walk out of here and you let a nigger stay," Philip said.

"You got a problem with me," Leonard said, "come to me and we'll sort it out."

"I'll sort it, all right," Philip said, and that's when he reached a little Saturday Night Special out from under the back of his shirt. "I'll put a hole in you, nigger."

Leonard lifted his hand quickly and then the knife was open in it. Philip lifted his gun to fire, and I don't know what came over me. Maybe it's the same thing that makes a soldier in combat leap on a grenade, but I stepped in front of Leonard and the bullet hit me in the chest at the same time Leonard's arm flicked over my shoulder and he let the knife go.

Next thing I know I'm on the floor, my head up against the bar. I felt strange and winded, as if I had been kicked in the chest. I could see Philip, Leonard's knife sticking out of his shoulder. He didn't seem to notice it there, but there was blood spreading around it, turning his light blue shirt dark. He pointed the gun in the direction of where I had last seen Shank.

The men at Philip's table were already on the floor, trying to make themselves as flat as pancakes.

The world roared. There was a rattling as shotgun pellets clattered around the room and picked some wood out of the table by Philip. Philip had blood spots all over him. He didn't go down though. He had lost his aim for a moment, but now he regained it. The little pistol barked a couple of times, and I heard a bottle break, and then I heard Shank say "shit," and then the Saturday Night Special barked two more times. I heard another bottle break and something heavy hit the floor behind the bar.

Fearfully, I touched my chest. I expected to touch a wet spot, but I only touched a tender spot.

Philip walked toward Leonard with the gun pointed at him. He pulled the trigger and it made a little snapping sound, but it didn't fire. He tried again with the same results.

Leonard had his fists up, but there was still too much space between him and Philip for him to throw a blow.

And then Philip said something I couldn't understand. A bubble of blood came out of his mouth like a chewing gum bubble. It popped apart, and Philip turned and walked toward the door, making each step with precision. He opened the door slowly and carefully, as if uncertain how it worked, went out and closed it politely behind him.

Leonard squatted down beside me and grabbed my shirt and ripped it open.

"You don't do that, Hap. You don't take shit for me, goddamn man, what is wrong with you?"

"I don't know," I said.

"You don't take a bullet for me, you dumb bastard. You just don't."

"I'd do it different, if I could," I said.

"Shit," Leonard said, looking at my chest. "It was a bad load. It just punched you. Shit, how about that? You are one lucky son of a bitch."

I looked down. A large bruise was forming, but the skin wasn't even broke.

Leonard helped me up. I felt better knowing I didn't have a hole in me. I went to the edge of the bar and looked behind it. Shank lay there with his eyes open. He was clutching a sawed-off double-barrel shotgun to his chest. A broken bottle of whiskey lay next to him, and it was mixing with the blood spreading across the floor from under his head. There was a perfect little hole in his face, just above the bridge of the nose.

I felt weak in the knees. Shank had caught the wrong bullet, and I had caught, at least from my viewpoint, the right one.

I started to tremble.

Leonard picked up the shotgun and cracked it open. It was empty. Shank had fired both shots at once.

"Damn," Leonard said. "What am I thinking?" He snatched up a rag from the bar and wiped the shotgun clean of his prints.

By this point the bar was empty. The door at the back was wide open and swinging in the wind.

We went out that way, and we could see a couple of the men from inside disappearing into the woods. We eased around the edge of the place and moved toward the front of it, and the lot where my car was parked. When we got there, we could see Philip.

He was at a Studebaker, and his back was to us. His chin was caught on the side mirror where he had fallen, and he was dangling from it, his knees almost touching the ground. His hands were open and there was something dark dripping from his fingers. I could see the little cheap-ass Saturday Night Special on the ground.

Leonard walked over and kicked the gun under the car. We both walked around and looked at Philip. His eyes were open, and the moon shone against them as if they were stagnant pond water.

Leonard reached out and took hold of his knife and pulled it from Philip's chest.

"Goddamn," I said, "you killed him."

"Don't be silly," Leonard said. "Shank's shotgun killed him. It just took a while."

Of course, the shotgun killed him, but the idea that during all that action Leonard had hit him with the knife amazed me. Philip's shirt was dark and wet with blood, and it was running down his arms and over his hands and fingers and dripping on the ground.

Lurking around the edge of the Watering Shack, we could see the men who had ran out the back door and into the woods. They quit lurking and hustled toward their cars, and before we could get to ours, they were starting theirs up, turning on lights, and roaring away.

We got in my Impala and I drove us out of there. The trees grew close to the road and dipped over us, and the shadows danced across the hood. I rolled a window down. I needed fresh air, and lots of it. I could hear the crickets sawing away as we went.

It was a couple days later that the news about the deaths at the Watering Shed showed up in the local newspaper.

Someone had found the bodies, probably whoever came out there the next night to drink beer.

The paper said the dead were Shank and Philip Atkins, and that was the first I knew of Philip's last name. It was thought they had killed each other in some kind of argument, which was accurate. It was noted that the Watering Shed had been subject to violence in the past. The paper also said no one had come forward with any information.

A year later, in the daytime, I drove out to Shank's by myself. In the harsh light of day, the place looked smaller and less mysterious than it had at night. It was funny how in that short bit of time the weather had worked the place over, ripped off a few sheets of the tin roof.

I walked to the front door and opened it and looked in. The back door was open and hung loosely by one hinge. Sunlight came through the gaps of missing tin from the roof. There were empty and broken bottles strewn about, and there was a pallet of some kind on the floor where some transient had made a nest. I went over to the bar and looked where Shank had lain. It was dark there. The blood and whiskey had turned black and had seeped into the wood floor. It looked like a varnish spill.

About a year later me and Leonard were in Marvel Creek, walking along the street, and a man passed us that I was certain was one of the men who had been playing cards with Philip. If he recognized us, he didn't let on, and we didn't make a thing of it either. We merely walked a little faster.

SPARRING PARTNER

"Once that bell rings you're on your own.
It's just you and the other guy."
—Joe Louis

THIS HAPPENED DURING SUMMER BREAK before I graduated high school.

Leonard found me at the end of the day when I had finished and stacked all the lumber and was putting up my tools. I was in a good mood because my employer owed me some nice money, and now I was done with a week's work and it was time to collect.

I was happy too because I had met a girl I liked. I met her at an out-of-town dance. But that is another story, and that girl, later in time, when me and Leonard were older, nearly got us killed. But right then I was thinking about her and how warm she had felt to dance with and the way we had touched, and later in my car, down a pine-bordered trail, we had parked and made love. She was not shy or hesitant about it, and up to that point it was the greatest moment of my life. I still rate it highly. It made me weak in the knees, and in time I realized it made me weak in the mind, but right then I was thinking good things about her, and sadly I knew I wouldn't see her next week, as she had gone out of town for a few days.

Leonard helped me put up my tools, which were an assortment of crowbars, hammers, and chisels.

It had been one hot, tough job, but the house wasn't too big, so all things considered, it had come down fast.

"What you up to?" he said.

I gave him a look.

"I'm putting up my fucking tools and you're helping me."

Leonard smiled at me. He had a very nice smile when he wanted to use it, and sometimes it could be fun and inviting and at other times it reminded you of a shark, right before its eyes rolled up in its head and its mouth opened wide and the teeth came together, with you between them.

"I got us a job," Leonard said.

"I just finished a job."

I closed up my box of tools.

"This is a good job."

"This was a good job. Not a career, but a good job."

"I got a better one doing something you and me are good at."

"What's that?"

"Knocking people down."

Me and Leonard had both been fighters, and in different ways. Leonard had been a fighter because he was black in a small town in deep East Texas during a time when Jim Crow was still alive and well, long after the time when slavery had been abolished, but the degradation of it had been kept alive: a soul-sucking day-to-day existence designed to remind a black person that they weren't on the same level as a white person, and that they were never going to be.

Leonard hadn't read that memo about how he should act, or maybe he had, but if so, he had torn it up and wiped his ass on it.

Me, I fought because a lot of people fought. It was damn near like a hobby in that little one-horse town, and the horse had a limp.

Later that day, after Leonard and I made plans to meet so he could tell me about the mysterious job, I got the money owed me, went home, ate a good dinner Mama had made. Sausage, spicy grits, and biscuits soft as clouds, tasty as ambrosia. Next morning, I drove out to meet Leonard on the black side of a town called LaBorde. It wasn't too far from where I lived in Marvel Creek. Years later, I would move there to live.

It was one of those days of summer when everywhere you went smelled like mowed grass and pine trees. The sun stayed bright for a long time, and the moon would come up in a thin wafer with the sun still in the sky. It was so beautiful it made me want to whistle and pull my dick.

As I drove into the black side of town, I saw young black men standing in ragged yards, or hunched on porches, as if those porches were their rafts in an awful churning ocean. They watched me drive by with cold eyes and stiff bodies. Nobody waved at me.

I stopped where Leonard was staying. The yard was nice and the house was well painted. It was a big house with a high porch and a kind of fenced-in crawl space. Leonard had parents, but he was staying with his Uncle Chester. They had their problems, he and his uncle, but there was no doubt in my mind that he was Leonard's true role model.

I parked at the curb, went up on the porch and knocked on the door. Next door there was a young black man with a bright red rag hanging out of his back pocket. He had a big-handled, black, wide-toothed comb buried in his bristling hairdo. He was about my age, strong-looking, with wide spaced front teeth, each of which seemed abnormally large.

He saw me and yelled out, "What you doing around here, white boy? You selling *Grit* door to door? Ain't nobody reads that shit. You ought to just pack on up and go before they don't find you no more."

Leonard came out of the house then, nearly knocking me over when he pushed the screen door back. He yelled to the kid on the porch.

"Come on over here, Lashawn."

"No, I'm all right."

"Come over here, goddamn it."

Lashawn's face lost its bright countenance. His mouth closed over his big teeth.

"Come on over here, I said."

Lashawn hesitated, came down off his porch and over to us, and up on the porch where we were. When Lashawn was close to Leonard, he touched the big comb in his hair. Up close I could see it was made of metal, and I could see Lashawn had got back some of his confidence, and he put it on display.

"You gonna get rough, Leonard, I'll cut your ass with this comb. It's a weapon."

Leonard hit Lashawn with a sharp jab that knocked him on his ass and made him do a somersault into the yard.

"What the fuck," Lashawn said, sitting up with a hand to his forehead where Leonard had popped him.

"Don't be talking to me like that. I done got a guest coming up in here, and you talking to him like he's a god-damn dog catcher."

Lashawn was still rubbing his head. "I didn't know he was a guest."

"He knocked on my door and is standing on my fuck-ing porch. You don't know much of any kind of shit, do you, Lashawn? Can't have you bad-mouthing my visitors. Right, Hap?"

"Well, I don't know. That was pretty harsh."

"Naw it wasn't," Leonard said. "Was it harsh, Lashawn?"

"Damn right it was. Wasn't no cause to hit me like that."

"I just gave you the cause. You deaf or just stupid? Why don't you go back over to your house and put some ice on your forehead? That's going to leave a knot. And you need to rearrange your comb."

When Lashawn went into his house, Leonard said, "I can't stand that country nigger. He's a goddamn thief. Can't abide a man that steals. Or wears a fucking comb in his hair."

"Aren't you from the country?"

"Yeah, but I'm sophisticated as poodle shit."

This event would be reminiscent of many in our future relationship.

We left there in Leonard's pickup, which rattled as it went, made a sound like a rod was loose and there needed to be a about two hundred dollars' worth of piston work. Leonard had a box of vanilla cookies setting between us, and now and again he'd dip his hand into the box and have one. He didn't offer me any.

I said, "Man, that was kind of unnecessary. He was just an asshole, not Attila the Hun."

"Way I see it I'm keeping him from growing up to be Attila. If not, motherfucker won't be Attila in my neighborhood."

I knew it was time to let the Lashawn discussion lay still.

"You say we got a job, but you haven't told me shit, except for that knocking people down part, and by the way, you like that better than I do, so do I really want to get in on this?"

"Thought I told you what it was, you might turn me down."

"I don't know I like a job that's a secret until you show it to me."

"Do you like four hundred dollars?"

"A piece?"

"No, split, but hell, two hundred dollars apiece, that's more than ass-wiping money."

Back then it sure was. Some people worked two, sometimes three or four weeks to make that much. Things were cheaper then, but cheap is relative.

"How much work?"

"A few partial days."

"Sounds too easy."

"Sometimes things are easy."

Leonard drove us into town and parked in front of a local café. "Let's get breakfast first."

"I don't know, Leonard."

"Mean 'cause blacks don't go in here? There ain't no law against it, you know. Lincoln freed the slaves."

"I don't know, man."

"I always wanted to try this place. I hear from some white folks it's good, and the cook is a cousin of mine."

"I don't know, man."

"You scared to go in there with a black man?"

"Yeah."

"Damn, really."

"Yeah. I'm scared what they might do to you. And I'm more scared what they might do to me. May not be a law on the books, but there's a kind of unspoken law."

"You hungry, ain't you?"

"Yeah. But I haven't been eating vanilla cookies. Where the hell do you put it all? How could you eat breakfast after all that?"

"With my precious little mouth."

"What say I get us some breakfast to go, bring it out to the truck."

"Don't insult my ass."

"I'm trying to save your ass. And mine."

"Well, you sit in the truck, and I'll go in and have breakfast, and I got something left over, like maybe a biscuit, I'll bring it out to you."

"Ah, Leonard."

He got out of the truck and was going up the steps and onto the sidewalk. I got out and walked after him, went in behind him. I think he wanted that to happen. For him to go in first.

There was a kind of buzz in the café and it smelled

of coffee and grease and toast, but when Leonard came in people quit talking and looked at us as if we had been made of tubercular spit and garbage.

Leonard said, "There's a booth, let's take that."

He said it loud.

We sat down at the booth, and both of us sat on the edge of our seats. Growing up where we grew up, we were wise enough not to end up trapped in a booth up against the wall. We weren't wise enough to stay outside.

People watched. Leonard waved at an old lady and her husband. A young man, a few years older than me, wearing a blue work cap, a khaki shirt and pants, work boots, got up and came over. He had a toothpick in his mouth, and he worked it from one side to the other. He stood at the booth, between me and Leonard, and looked down at Leonard.

Leonard isn't a moose, but he's a tall, solid guy and he was tough. We had trained in boxing together, and I had started taking martial arts at the Tyler YMCA twice a week most weeks, and I was teaching him what I knew, as a black person would get nothing but the runaround if he tried to sign up for class. The true nature of *budo* at the YMCA was you best be white.

"Ain't you in the wrong café?" the young man said, dropping his chin a little.

Leonard looked around, then up at the man. "I don't think so. How's the breakfast here?"

"If you're white, it tastes pretty good."

"Yeah, what if you're black?"

"You don't get to taste it."

"Who's going to stop me? You?"

"Me, maybe some others. Maybe all at once."

"You know what?"

"What?"

"I wouldn't count on it."

The white man smiled a little, then looked at me. "What you doing hanging around with him?"

"I work for him. He gives me a dollar at the end of the day, though I still got to shine his shoes."

"Yeah?"

"Yeah," Leonard answered for me. "I'm teaching him to be a nigger in ten easy lessons."

"You're a smart ass, aren't you?"

"Better than a dumb ass."

"You're looking for trouble, colored boy."

"You call an alligator a lizard? Don't call me boy."

The man opened his mouth to say it again, but Leonard said, "I wouldn't."

The man looked at me. "You backing his play?"

"All the way."

Leonard glanced at me and smiled, and then he turned and stared at the man, and Leonard's face changed. His eyes turned sharklike, like I was talking about, and his mouth made a smile that sent a chill up my back.

"You want to play, white boy?" Leonard said.

"You need to stay out of here," the man said. "It ain't right."

"I got the message, considered it, discarded it."

The man started walking away. "It ain't right."

No one else moved. Leonard stared at all of them. As for me, all I could do was sit there and feel my ankles vibrate a little in my work boots. I had crossed the color line and I had to decide. Walk and go my way and be safe, or protect my newfound friend. The thought of leaving was there, but it passed quickly.

I called to a middle-aged waitress, "Ma'am. We need some service, please."

She hesitated, looked around and walked away, disappeared behind the counter and went into the back. When she came back, a big black man wearing a white, food-spotted apron and a white cap was with her. He came over and said, "Leonard, you crazy?"

Leonard said, "Yep. This here is my buddy, Hap. Hap, this is my cousin, Simon. He is a very safe kind of man."

"Hey," I said.

"Damn, man, you crazier than Leonard. You ain't going to cruise the world like you did before, not after this. You know that?"

"Crossed my mind."

"You our waitress?" Leonard said.

Simon studied Leonard, then sighed gently, like that was all the air he had left in him.

"Someday it's all going to catch up with you, way you are around white folks. You got to know how the game is played, and you're playing it wrong."

"No. You're playing it wrong."

"What we'll have is a menu," I said, all of a sudden feeling my oats.

Simon stood there for a long moment. We could hear muttering in the crowd. Someone said nigger under their breath. It wasn't the same as when Leonard said it.

"I heard that," Leonard said. "I'm putting you on my list."

Things got quiet.

Simon went away, came back carrying two menus. "Okay, there ain't no law says you have to leave, but another law's going to catch up with you. White man's invisible law."

"And there's that whole God's law too about us queers."

"Oh, God, don't bring that up. That there is not a law to be broken by man or woman, white or black. God has his rules."

"Does he?" Leonard said.

Simon gave us the menus.

"What the hell do you want? Let's get this over with."

Leonard studied the menu, said, "They got corn muffins on here for breakfast."

"I think I'll try one," I said. "Make it two and a cup of coffee."

"Corn muffins for breakfast, Hap? What the hell?"

"They're new," Simon said.

"Say they are," Leonard said. "What they like?"

"Cornbread," Simon said.

"Cornbread. Hell, for breakfast? I don't want no cornbread for breakfast. I was having lunch, had some pinto beans to go with it, some collards, I'd be in, but corn muffins for breakfast? What the hell, man?"

"I don't make the menu."

"You can eat whatever you want for breakfast, Leonard," I said.

"I know that, and I will, but it won't be no corn muffin. Give me some scrambled eggs with some of that homemade hot sauce I know you got 'cause my friend Linson's mother makes it for here, and give me an order of sausage and four pieces of toast, some jam or jelly of some sort, and while you're back there, make sure no one spits in my food, and that means you too."

"Goodness, Leonard," Simon said, took the menus and went away fast.

We didn't get glasses of water, but while we waited on the food, a man leaned out from the booth behind us.

He looked about forty, a rough forty, had on work clothes and a weathered gray cap. He looked as if he went to bed tired and woke up tired, and with that cap on.

"You're right about them cornbread muffins. Who the hell eats those for breakfast?"

"What I was saying," Leonard said.

"And they have the lunch, they don't serve them then. And who the hell calls dinner lunch? Next thing they'll call supper dinner."

"They do that up North," I said.

"Well, there you go. Up North they got a lot of funny

ideas. But the thing I was saying is it's bad enough they don't know the name of the meals, but you order pintos, you get some light bread with it. I say you can make a corn muffin in the morning, you can damn sure make one at dinner, and not serve some damn tasteless light bread with pintos."

Leonard nodded. "It's the same ingredients. Right?"

"You know," said an elderly man sitting with an elderly blue-haired woman at a table near us, "you're right. I'm going to go talk to them."

The man got up and went to the back. He seemed quite determined. When he returned, he sat down, said, "They say they're going to put the muffins on the lunch menu, but they're going to leave them on the breakfast menu, 'cause some people like them. Can you believe that?"

"I'm going to try them," I said.

No one seemed interested in what I was going to try.

"That Simon," said the man at the table, "he sure can cook."

"He don't put enough bacon in the beans, though," said the blue-haired woman. "He skimps on that."

"Maybe that's the management," said the man in the booth next to us. "I mean, they got to be the ones came up with cornbread for breakfast, so maybe they skimp on the bacon."

He was still leaning out. Cornbread muffins seemed very important to him.

I had often had slices of cornbread with syrup for breakfast, and bet some of them had, but maybe because it was in muffin form, they felt it was all wrong. I decided not to bring that up.

"Well now, y'all enjoy your breakfast," Leonard said.

"You too," said the man in the booth. "What's that them frogs in France say. Bone up a tit."

"I don't think that's exactly it," I said.

"Close enough," Leonard said. "Bone up a tit."

The cornbread muffins with butter and jam were good, and I ate them a little fast and slurped my coffee down, wanting to get out of there. When Simon came around with the check, which he had written out quickly, Leonard asked for more coffee, so I said I should have some too. I didn't want it, but Simon poured it. I drank it black, and it made me more nervous than I already was.

Leonard sopped up his well-peppered eggs with the toast and took his time about it all. When we finished, he pushed the check over to me.

"Why don't you take care of that, Hap, you done got all that big money."

I took the check, and Leonard paid the tip. I noticed he put a big tip on the table. I got up and went to the cash register. Leonard went over to the elderly couple and asked the lady how much bacon she put in her pintos and they shared a recipe or two, like maybe they were planning a picnic or some such.

The woman behind the register was the waitress who wouldn't wait on us. She took my money and said to me so she couldn't be heard.

"I couldn't wait on you two, 'cause I did, it would be the end of my job."

"I know," I said.

"But I got to say, things didn't go like I thought they would."

"Me either," I said, and I was happy about it.

She gave me some change and I gave her a dollar of it for no real reason at all, went over and got Leonard by the elbow and started us out of there.

The elderly woman said, "I always put a bit of lard and a touch of sugar in there with my bacon."

"That's because you know what you're doing," Leonard said, and she smiled her false teeth at him.

It was starting to turn rain-cloud dark as we drove out into the deep country, and tooled along the back roads where shacks seemed to be more thrown up than built. There were more black people on porches, mainly kids and old people, and they were watching us drive by, a salt-and-pepper job in a time when those human condiments didn't much exist on the same table in the South.

Finally, we went down a narrow country road of red

clay, snaked along between the trees as the rain clouds continued to gather and the shadows swelled and covered the road in darkness that was sliced only by bits of cloud-muted sunlight. That's the thing about East Texas. Sunny one moment, raining the next.

"How's that girl you seeing?" Leonard said.

"Haven't seen her that much, but it's going good, I think. She's out of town for a few days with her parents."

"Yeah?"

"Yeah."

"I got a feeling you done whipped, Hap. I ain't known you that long, but I know you like that stuff like a hound dog likes a pork chop."

"It's good stuff."

"I wouldn't know. Queer niggers ain't popular around here, and other queers, white or black, they kind of stay silent. For me it's whacking off to the men's section of the Sears catalogue."

A year back one of the kids in our school, younger than me, Sammy Lean, had paid some kids to let him suck their dicks. They took the money and let him do the deed, and then they beat him up. After, they told him he had more money, he could suck them again, but each time a beating would come with it. I heard they did that two or three times, and finally Sammy had been humiliated enough. During a dark night he hung himself with a jump rope from the Sabine Bridge in Marvel Creek.

He wasn't found for three days. A fisherman in a boat

looked up and saw him dangling. He had bitten through his tongue, almost severing it. He had died fully dressed but with his dick hanging out. He had painted it bright red with spray paint. Or so it was said. There were suspicions he might not actually have hung himself, or owned the paint that decorated his pecker. But after a few laughs from the kids he had been paying, and a brief investigation by the police, which amounted to a fifteen-minute query with his parents and a slap on the back for the kids that he had paid for sex, Sammy and his red dick were buried out of town with all the ceremony of a backyard cat funeral. His parents moved away, more shamed by his death than grieved.

How the hell Leonard survived in that time and climate, bold about his blackness and his sexuality, is beyond me, but it not only made him tough, I think it made him damaged. Darkness crawled around inside of him, and sometimes showed itself in his eyes. Later, he would add the Vietnam War to that.

When we arrived at our destination, it was raining fiercely. The place was a large barn out in the woods off a trail barely wide enough for a car, the trees tight on either side. There had been a house not far from the barn, but it had burned down and all that was left of it was a chimney and some burnt wood, and possibly the mineral rights.

"What the hell, Leonard?"

"It's all right. Come on."

Leonard parked near the barn, and we got out in the

rain and pushed the barn doors open and went inside. There was a boxing ring put together on a platform in the middle of the barn. There was a young black man in the ring with an older black man, and he was knocking the kid around like he was a paddleball.

"Cover up," a big black man at the edge of the ring was yelling. "Cover up, you stupid son of a bitch."

There were a dozen other black men standing around, assorted in ages and sizes, but all of them had the same look now, one of surprise as we came in. But their focus wasn't on Leonard, it was on me.

"Leonard," the big black man who had been doing the yelling said. "What the fuck is this?"

"It's a guy named Hap," Leonard said.

"He's white."

"Oh. Shit. You're right."

Leonard kept walking and I kept walking with him, but I won't josh you. I was starting to feel nervous. More so than in the café.

"You said you'd bring me a sparring partner," the big black man said.

We were standing by the ring.

"Listen here, Bus. Said I'd bring someone with me to help you train your guy. This is that someone. Me and him, we can train your boy, but we can't give him left tit. He has to have that already."

"I don't know what all he's got. Just know he's got a hell of a hook, no footwork, and he gets hit a lot. But when he makes contact, sounds like two cars running together, and I hear the angels' harps playing."

"Is that him?" I said, nodding at the kid in the ring.

"No, this is Will, and he's someone I'm teaching to be a sparring partner. Right now, I think he's starting to regret it."

"Got that right," said the young man in the ring. He grabbed a towel hanging over the ropes, wiped his face with it, slipped through the ropes, and dropped to the ground.

"I don't think I want to be a sparring partner no more," he said, and started walking away.

Bus yelled to the kid as he headed out of the barn. "You couldn't be a boxer if they spread your ass with salad spoons and stuck Sugar Ray Robinson up there."

"You got that right," said the man at ringside who had been yelling for Will to cover up.

"This boy you got, me and Hap can show him some footwork, teach him to cover up."

"What I need," Bus said, "is sparring partners for him, someone won't get knocked down or out first time they get in the ring. You calling him a boy, that's your choice. How old are you, and this cracker? What's he? Twelve."

"Thirteen, sir," I said.

"Oh, good, a wise-ass white boy," said Bus. "You know how much I like that, ain't that right, Dixie?"

He was speaking to the man who had told the young man to cover up. He had a big belly and wore a white T-shirt that might have fit him at birth but now was straining over his gut. For the record, it was more of a pinto-colored shirt. There were tobacco spit stains on it, and I think the stain on the loose neck of the shirt was maybe cheese, possibly mustard. I decided on mustard.

"Yeah, you love that shit," Dixie said. "Me and you both."

"Hap's all right," Leonard said. "Just got a mouth sometime."

"Choice," said Dixie. "I like that, coming from you."

"I need someone better than alright," Bus said.

Dixie said, "Joe, come over here."

About this time one of the men in the crowd, an acne-scarred black man who I judged to be in his late twenties, early thirties, came over. His shoulders rolled from side to side as he walked, and his chin was slightly down, as if he were about to rest it on his chest.

Bus said, "This here is one of my fighters, he's seven and one, and that one he lost was on a technicality. But the guy he lost to couldn't get a job sorting socks now, beating he took."

Joe looked me up and down. "Shit. Sparring partner. This honky looks more like a punching bag."

"Take it easy, Joe," Leonard said. "Or you might wake up with a crowd around you."

"Man, you got some faith in this cracker?" Joe said. "What are you doing here, peckerwood? On break from kindergarten?"

"I'd stop if I were you," Leonard said.

By now all the men, young and old, had gathered around us. Joe was looking me up and down. "Naw. He ain't much."

"Have it your way," Leonard said.

Joe grinned, said, "I think a strong wind would blow white boy down."

"It would have to be a really strong one," I said.

Joe reached out to push a hand against my chest, said, "Let's see what it takes."

I slapped his hand aside, stepped in, and hit him with an upper cut under the chin so solid it lifted him on his toes, and then he dropped on the dirt floor. All he needed then was a blankie and a teddy bear to snuggle with, possibly a surgeon to open his head and put a new brain in it.

Bus looked down at Joe. Blood was filling up in his open mouth. Bus bent down and turned his head so the blood would flow out on the ground and not down his throat.

All the other black men came over to look at Joe napping.

"Man," said Dixie. "I believe that nigger is trying to row a boat over River Jordan."

Leonard laughed a little. "That there is my boy, Hap. Got another one you want knocked down, set him up."

Bus studied me. "I reckon you'll do."

Me and Leonard were still on the floor near the ring, and I was sitting on a stool, and he was pulling boxing gloves onto my wrapped hands. I was still wearing my jeans, but I'd taken my shirt and shoes and socks off.

"This tough guy they got," Leonard said. "He's just another tomato can, you see. All Bus's guys are tomato cans. He keeps a steady shelf of them so he can pull down one when he needs it. He only wants this one to get a bit of learning so he can last longer, make Bus some money on bets."

"He said he had a good hook."

Leonard was lacing up my gloves, pulling the strings tight.

"I know what he said, but I know Bus. He only does so much work on a fighter, only gives Dixie so much time with them, then a new nigger's up. He had a peckerwood once, Jimmy Oasis they called him, on account of they couldn't pronounce the last name. He became Oasis. And that guy could fight, until he couldn't. Got so someone closed their fist, he was starting to faint. Bus pushed him too fast and too hard. He could have been good, but Bus ruined him."

"I haven't ever been a sparring partner."

"Now you will be."

"You seen or fought this guy Bus has?"

"Nope. But Bus thinks maybe this fucker might be his meal ticket. A real boxer who might even fight another real boxer and go big-time."

"Thought you said Bus is small potatoes, burns fighters out?"

"Well, from what I hear, it might take some real fire to burn this guy out. What he lacks in skill he makes up for it in having the brain of a dinosaur. Bus is hoping he'll get some local championships out of him, maybe get a well-paying fight. You can bet, whatever the purse is, it'll be Bus pulling the purse strings, and the guy wins, he'll end up with chewing gum money, and Bus will keep pushing him, not preparing him. He just wants his boxer to quit blocking with his face. You're ready."

"Where's the fighter?"

"I don't know. Let's ask."

We walked over to where Bus was leaning on the platform for the ring.

"Where's your boxer?" Leonard said.

"He's in the back," Bus said, "getting his muscles stretched, getting oiled down some. And they're trying to find some shorts big enough for him to put his balls in."

"I didn't get to stretch," I said. "I don't have a mouthpiece or a cup."

Bus said, "Ain't got no cups or mouthpieces, and shit, who wants to share. Should have brought your own. Do a couple knee bends, swing your arms a little. You'll be all right. And you look like you have plenty of room for your balls."

"I'm wearing jeans, shouldn't I at least get some shorts?"

"You don't want the ones they got back there," Leonard

said. "No telling whose ass has been in them and when they were last washed. That shared junk is a chocolate party."

"Can't disagree with that," Bus said.

That's when the fellows on the floor near the ring stood up and looked to the rear of the barn. Out of a room on the side came a black man shiny from a fresh rubdown, about six-four, with shoulders wide enough and thick enough you could have laid a picnic table across them. His stomach was flat and his head was large, resembled a block of granite.

"Goddamn," I said to Leonard.

"Yeah, well, he's bigger than I expected. Keep your hands up."

The guy came over to stand by Bus. He punched one gloved hand into the other, like he was kneading bread dough.

"Which one of these fools is going to show me some footwork?" the fighter said.

"The fool wearing the gloves," Bus said.

"Yeah," the fighter said, "thought it was him."

"This here," Bus said, "is my fighter. We call him the Man Slayer."

"Wow," Leonard said. "Cool nickname. Listen here, Bus, this fella is way bigger than Hap."

"You noticed," Bus said. "White boy's big enough. They ain't fighting for the fucking title. You worried about his height, Leonard, you can stand him on a stool."

"That's nice of you," I said.

Leonard talked them into letting me go to the dressing room so he could help me stretch.

"Listen here," Leonard said, "I didn't know this guy was going to be the Jolly Black Fucking Giant. You want out, I can get you out. Shit, we can go through the window there, be gone by the time Man Slayer figures out how to climb in the ring."

"In for a penny, in for a pound."

"Good news is you're getting more than a penny."

"Yeah, well, I hope I'm in the condition to spend it afterwards."

"Out-footwork the motherfucker. Looks to me his ribs would be a good target with hooks."

"You mean because I can't reach his head."

"Yeah, what I was thinking. You're just supposed to give him a workout, but Bus, he has his boys wear their sparring partners pretty hard. He's not worrying about your fucking health. He wants his boy to have a punching bag, so you play this like it's a fucking title bout."

"Seems to me you know a lot more about this than you told me."

"I needed the money, but hey, so do you."

"I got some money."

"After a few days, you'll have even more money. Maybe a nice funeral, with a wreath."

We went out and I climbed in the ring with the big guy. He looked at me the way a snake looks at a mouse it's decided on for dinner.

"Watch him, Man Slayer," Bus said. "White boy here knocked Joe on his ass with one punch."

Joe was awake now and was sitting in a chair in the front row rubbing his jaw. "He caught me by surprise."

Leonard was up on the platform, outside the ropes by my corner. I sat down on the stool in the ring to think about what kind of plans my folks might have for my body.

Leonard said to Joe, "He caught you by surprise all right, but if he had sounded a siren and flashed some lights and called you by name, he'd still have knocked you on your fat ass. You was playing all bad and shit, pushing on Hap, and he knocked your little train off the tracks."

"I'll get you, Leonard," Joe said.

"No, you won't," Leonard said. "They'll find you in some weeds out back of this barn."

"That's enough tough talk," Dixie said, climbing up on the platform. "That's plenty, even if you got more to go around. And I know you do, Leonard."

"I got enough everyone here can share a bit of it," Leonard said.

Dixie climbed into the ring and came over to me. "Look here, this is Bus's boy, but he fights dirty because that's how Bus taught him. He'll try to hook your balls or thumb your eye, rub his laces across your face. He's big and looks dumb, but he's not. But that don't make him a boxer. He winds up and throws haymakers. He's got a hook that could knock a fart out of a rhino's ass, but if you got any footwork at all, you can probably stay out of range. But he gets your ass in a corner, he can do some damage, that hook, you know. Gets you cornered, you better cover up, 'cause that hook gets your head a time or two, you'll be lucky you got enough brain left to get a job sacking groceries on crutches."

"Okay," I said.

"Okay my ass, white boy. You pay attention."

"I didn't exactly think you were on my side."

"You in my corner, ain't you? You move and stick with a jab. Bus, he don't have me teach no jabs much. He's all for getting in there and throwing hammers. You can't throw a hammer, you got to use a razor, hear me?"

"Yes, sir."

"All right, then. Listen here, you get carried out, wake up on the floor over there, like Joe did, there ain't no shame in it."

"Don't over-encourage me," I said.

Bus was over in the corner with Man Slayer, holding one of his wrists in each hand, shaking them. I heard him say, "Don't take it too easy. Don't go easy at all."

"I won't," Man Slayer said.

"Sitting right here," I said.

They looked at me and grinned as Leonard leaned over the ropes and Dixie climbed through them and stood out on the platform at the edge of the ring.

"Hey, brother," Leonard said. "I got your back. Look here. I think that motherfucker looks in better shape than he is. Make him work for it."

"You think he looks in better shape than he is? What kind of evaluation is that?"

Someone banged a bell. I stood up, and Leonard reached through the ropes and took my stool away. Man Slayer moved into the ring like a bull that was about to mount a cow. I got on my bicycle a little, started shuffle-stepping around, making Man Slayer chase me.

"Cut him off," Bus was yelling. "Corner his ass."

Man Slayer was too slow to corner my ass. I kept shuffling.

Bus said, "You get in there and punch some, you goddamn cracker. Ain't paying you to cut a fucking rug."

That's when I skipped in and jabbed Man Slayer in the nose. It wasn't a hard jab, but Man Slayer started bleeding right off.

"It's all right," Bus said to him. "You ain't hurt."

Man Slayer touched his bleeding nose with his glove, gave Bus a look that indicated he might think otherwise.

"You're all right," Bus said. "Shake it the fuck off. Knock him on his ass. Blow right through him."

"All right?" Leonard called to Bus from across the ring, "That motherfucker's bleeding like he's on the rag. What you mean he's all right?"

"Shake that shit off," Bus said to his fighter.

"Everybody shut up," Dixie said.

Man Slayer was mad now, and he came at me running. I sidestepped a little, hooked him with a left to the ribs, and that made him blow out his air. I turned then and hit him with an overhead right in the jaw. I had to go up on my toes to reach him.

His head moved slightly, and then he looked back at me. I thought, Oh hell.

But that look of fire and ice didn't stay long. Man Slayer's eyes glazed over and he stumbled a little, tried to hit me with his famous hook, but he might as well have been offering me his hand to dance. I ducked under that easily. I could have stopped and had a cup of coffee before that fist got to me. I caught him in the ribs again, and when I did, he bent over, and I caught him with my right again, this time in the temple. As he tried to pick his head up, pull his hands in front of him, I slipped an uppercut through his arms and caught him on the center of his chin. It was like someone turned out his lights. He fell over and lay on the floor of the ring in a fetal position and wiggled a little. Slowly his legs stretched out and he quit moving.

"Goddamn," Joe said, standing up from his chair. "Son of a bitch did it again."

I bent over Man Slayer, and shook his shoulders with my gloves. One of his eyes flickered, like someone was trying to raise a window shade, then the shade went back down and lay heavy over his eye.

Dixie and Bus came into the ring, went over to make sure Man Slayer was all right. I hoped he was. When I hit him, I could feel the electricity of that uppercut from my fist all the way down to my toes, and on point of impact, my balls tingled like the vibration from church bells.

I climbed through the ropes and Leonard started taking the gloves off of my hands.

"Shit, Hap. Hit that fucker any harder, they'd have to put a monkey and some Tang on board with him so he could circle the fucking moon."

Joe came over and looked up at me.

"All right. I'll say it. You damn sure know how to knock a brother out."

When Man Slayer got some ammonia under his nose and they brought him around, Bus and Dixie got him on his feet and helped him get through the ropes and down on the floor. Bus and Joe helped Man Slayer stagger back to the dressing room without falling over.

Dixie came down from the ring and walked over to us.

Leonard said, "Tomorrow, it's my turn."

"You ain't coming back tomorrow," Dixie said.

"What the hell you mean? You wanted sparring partners, so here we are."

"Yeah, well, he wanted some stiffs, and Hap here, he ain't no stiff."

"Nah, he ain't," Leonard said. "And I ain't neither. Was you thinking I was a stiff?"

"What I'm thinking," Dixie said, "is Man Slayer ought to change his name to the Marvel Creek Bleeder. I told Bus he wasn't no good against someone with some skills, a dancing master, a jabber. Bus thought his size would overwhelm whoever was out there."

"He is big," I said, "and for the record, he scared me pretty good."

"Scaring you didn't do him no good," Dixie said. "For him to win, he's got to hit somebody. Only way he'd have hit you solid is if you were tied to a tree."

Dixie took out his wallet and gave me and Leonard two hundred dollars apiece. That was a lot of money for one round and a knockout.

"Hey, man," Leonard said. "I don't want to look a gift horse in the mouth, but this is more than I agreed to for one day. I figured we'd have to go a week or two for this much."

"Rest of that is so you don't go around town saying how bad a boxer Bus has."

"I was you," Leonard said, "I wouldn't put the gloves on that ox again. I'd maybe get him some kind of job hauling bricks or some such. Otherwise, you might ought to just go on and order him a tombstone and buy a burial plot and order the flowers."

Dixie nodded, and me and Leonard went out of there with our money and no more job.

I was having an early breakfast one Saturday, munching on homemade cinnamon rolls, hot sauce grits and gravy, sipping coffee, watching my dad sitting across from me at the table, finishing up his breakfast. He had a saucer, and he put a tablespoon of Brer Rabbit Syrup and a tablespoon of butter in it, and was tipping hot coffee from his cup onto the saucer. It melted the butter and spread the syrup. He used a piece of toast to sop it up. The phone rang.

Daddy was closer to it, and all he had to do was reach out and pull it out of its rack on the wall. He answered briskly, put the phone down on the table, said, "For you. Sounds like a nigger."

I got up and went around the table and picked up the phone. Dad took a last sip of coffee, got up and said, "Going to work," and then he was out the door.

I put the phone to my ear and said, "It's Hap."

"Surprise, it is a nigger."

"Shit, Leonard. Sorry you heard that."

"Like I don't know there's people call me that. I don't like it, but it's not like it's some kind of surprise. I say it's all right, by the way."

"What you keep telling me."

"I got something for you. Remember that job as sparring partners we had?"

"Of course."

"Well, they want us back."

"Nope."

"Look here, you're not going to believe this. They're offering us a hundred a day."

"No one has money like that."

"You mean no one black has money like that."

"I didn't say that."

"But you were thinking it."

"Leonard, we don't have money like that. I don't know anybody that can pay us a hundred apiece to go in and dance around with some half-ass boxer."

"They got a new boy, and they think he's got something. He has all the moves."

"That so," I said.

"Yep. Lot of money, man."

I considered. I still had some of the money we had been given by Dixie, as well as some stash from the job I'd finished, but some of it had gone for jeans and union shirts I had tie-dyed, and I had a new pair of desert boots, as we were calling them then. I had bought a bunch of paperbacks off a drugstore rack. Replenishing of funds would be nice.

"We'll get hit a lot," I said.

"Didn't get hit so much last time."

"Yeah, but this is supposed to be their new badass."

"True," Leonard said. "But hey, we got some moves."

"We like to think we do," I said.

"Don't be modest and I won't."

"Are you ever?" I said.

It was a dry, hot day when we drove out to the boxing barn again. We got out of my car carrying boxing trunks and boxing shoes wrapped up in towels, had them tucked under our arms. Leonard had driven to Tyler the day before and had got us some jocks and cups and mouthpieces. He gave me mine.

"You were pretty confident I'd be back, buying this stuff," I said.

"Just pretend you got something to put in that cup," he said.

Inside the barn a big swamp cooler had been set in a window and it was beating the air without much success. Way it whined from time to time, I thought it might back out of the window and run off.

The crowd was smaller this time. Dixie, Bus, and Joe, who had the air of retirement about him, and a white guy we hadn't seen before, along with this tall, lanky, good-looking, brown kid with close-cropped hair. He was wearing new, white boxing shorts and white boxing shoes. They were all standing inside the raised ring. The boxer was a little shiny, like he'd just gone a few rounds of shadow boxing. I didn't see another fighter there, so I took that to be the case, like he had been showing his moves against the air. The air is a favored opponent.

Bus and the white guy were both wearing sports shirts and slacks and sports jackets, and the white guy had on sunglasses. There were bands of speckled lightbulbs hung across the ceiling, and light also came through in alternating blades of the swamp cooler. It wasn't a place you needed sunglasses.

This white guy's hair was cut close and it was graying and prickly looking. He had a belly pushing against a nylon pullover shirt with a collar that was blue and white and draped by a plaid sports jacket. His face had a banged around look. Dad always said a guy that has a tough face isn't any more than a guy that can't keep his hands up. Guy gave him that face, that's your boy, he said.

Still, he wasn't a guy I wanted any part of. There was an air about him of a guy that would steal a child's orthopedic shoes.

Bus had on a nice, dark sports jacket and slacks and a button-up white shirt, but he was the kind of guy that would always look like what he wore was supposed to fit someone else. Yet, him being dressed up meant something, I figured, like he was trying to impress the cracker in sunglasses.

Dixie's T-shirt had a different arrangement of stains this day.

The young man in boxing trunks and boxing shoes

looked down at me in a slightly surprised way. Dixie saw him looking, said, "Ty, Hap looks like a hippie, but he can hit. I bet if he or Leonard wanted, I could turn them both into fighters."

Bus turned his attention to us.

"I've had Dixie working the kid here, Ty, but he might need some harder hitters, some quicker hands to deal with. Some guy like you rides the bicycle."

He was indicating me, of course, and it was meant to be something of an insult, something to explain his fighter Man Slayer getting knocked on his ass. Like I had ran from him until he knocked himself out.

Leonard said, "Ought to change your man's name from Man Slayer to Likes to Get Knocked the Fuck Out."

"Don't pay him no mind," Bus said. "He don't know nothing."

"He knows a little," Dixie said, and grinned.

I was starting to like Dixie.

"Man Slayer has moved on," Bus said.

"I bet," Leonard said. "What about Joe here?"

"I'm on what they call hiatus," Joe said. "See you fellows."

Joe climbed through the ring, dropped to the floor, and moved back toward the dressing room, and we never saw him again. He either went out the back door or is still in the dressing room trying to decide which side of his shorts go in front.

Anyway, while Joe was walking to the dressing room,

we all watched him go like we were observing the departure of the last of the dodos.

The white guy still hadn't said a word.

Leonard studied the white man, said, "What the fuck is he, a deaf mute?"

"He finances," Bus said.

"What's he finance?"

"Fights," Bus said.

The white man slowly smiled and spoke. His voice was surprisingly high, like a eunuch's in the Venetian choir. "Had a black boy talked smart to me once. High school boy like you. Word is he got set on fire."

"Try setting me on fire, motherfucker," Leonard said.

I watched to see if Bus and Dixie were going to turn on this white guy, talking like that, but they didn't. They just looked uncomfortable, like they were in the midst of a rectal exam and the doctor had just announced he'd found a dick broken off in there.

The white man's face was as unmoving as one of the faces on Mount Rushmore, but his fingers clenched slightly where they rested against his legs. He looked at Leonard for a long time. "Me and the shine here got to go," said the white man.

Bus cleared his throat and the two of them climbed through the ropes on the other side of the ring and started walking across the barn in the direction Joe had taken.

"Bus fixing to give whitey a back rub, maybe a quick hand job?" Leonard said.

"Keep it down," Dixie said. "That's trouble you don't need. I sure don't need it. And Bus, he's a dick, but he don't need it from that honky neither. No offense, Hap."

"None taken."

"That peckerwood knows some fellas that know some fellas, if you know what I mean."

"No, I don't know what you mean," Leonard said. "That milky motherfucker looks like someone that doesn't know shit from wild honey to me. And this guy. What the name again? Ty? He's your fighter."

Ty dipped his head, like the most important thing for him to do was to examine the canvas and see if ants might be crossing it caravan style.

"What the fuck's going on here?" Leonard said.

"It's complicated," Dixie said. "Thing is, ain't neither of you need to worry your pretty little heads about it. Go back there and get dressed. And you, Hap, you put the gloves on."

"Ain't I going to get to hit nobody?" Leonard said.

"Somebody," I said. "You can't hit nobody."

"I'm trying to bottom out with the atmosphere here, man. Getting in the common language groove."

"Well pardon me all to hell," I said.

"What the fuck are you guys chattering about?" Dixie said.

"They're discussing diction," Ty said, finally raising his head. He had a nice mellow voice, and he gave us a slight grin.

"Listen to the man," Leonard said. "He knows of which he speaks."

"The rain in Spain stays mainly in the plain," Ty said.

Leonard was wrapping my hands. He hadn't bothered to put on his shorts and shoes, as I was the one Dixie had asked for.

"Asked you up first 'cause they want to see if he can corner you, case whoever he fights is a dancer too."

"Anything but the polka," I said.

"Thing is, Dixie, he ain't quite the dick Bus is, but they probably want the kid to come on hard, so it'll be more than a sparring match. I suggest you don't knock him on his ass right away, earn some time and we'll make more money, we can stretch this out a few days."

"What if I can't knock him on his ass?"

"I guess it'll work out for me either way."

"That's sweet. What do you think about Mr. Sunglasses?"

"Some big ass trying to make money off black folks' hides and call it sport. My figure is Bus and Whitey are going someplace where Whitey can tell Bus how he better muzzle me, or me and Bus are going to end up in a ditch someplace."

"Maybe you ought to quiet it down some."

"Not my nature."

It was really a light time in the ring, and Ty didn't try to take any cheap shots against me. He looked pretty, was quick on his feet, had fast punches, but I knew something right off. He couldn't crack an egg with either hand even if he was hungry.

Because of that, I flicked him with a jab a lot, but didn't let it clobber him. I threw some light crosses and hooks and he dodged a few. He ought to have. I threw them slower than usual. Even a man blind in one eye with his back foot in a bucket of cement could have slipped or padded them off.

When we finished, I came down out of the ring, and Leonard handed me my towel. I wiped the sweat off me as best I could. It wasn't like they had a shower at the barn. They barely had a working toilet.

Ty climbed through the ropes and came down out of the ring and smiled at me. "Thanks, man. You move quick."

"Thanks, Ty," I said, and Ty went away whistling toward the back to change.

Dixie climbed down out of the ring.

"Only thing you didn't do in there was give the kid a kiss and a dozen roses."

"You hired me to work him, not knock him down," I said.

"Ty's got some moves," Leonard said, "but they're mostly for the dance studio."

"Bus don't think so," Dixie said.

"Bus don't give a shit," Leonard said. "He'd put an infant in the ring if they could fit the gloves."

"He's not so bad," Dixie said.

"Yeah he is," Leonard said. "Looking pretty, having the moves, doesn't make you fighter."

"Yeah, well," Dixie said. "Gonna help Ty get those gloves off. Can you come back in a couple hours, give him another round? Leonard this time."

We agreed we could.

Dixie nodded and started toward the back.

"Give them a minute before you go back and change," Leonard said.

"All right. Hey, it's odd, but Ty, he can't hit any harder than a paralyzed grandma. You see that one he caught me with. He punches to you, not through you."

"Thought that looked like the case. He's got the shoulder launch, the hip switch, but you can see it's a butterfly."

"Float like a butterfly and sting like a moth," I said.

When me and Leonard finally went to the back, Ty was still there. He was sitting alone in the dressing room on a wooden bench.

"You got some moves," he said to me.

"Thanks."

"I can't do the kind of footwork you do. I mean, I got footwork, but it's not helping that much."

"That's because you got footwork for footwork's sake," Leonard said. "You got to have a reason to shuffle, to step and lunge, to skip on back or to the side. You're just moving around, Ty."

"I know it."

"How did you get into this?" Leonard said.

"One of them things, you know. How old are you guys?" We told him.

"You look my age."

"Which is?" Leonard said.

"Twenty-one."

"Yeah, well, you just got a few years on us," Leonard said.

"So, you're sitting at home, and one day you jump up and decide to be a boxer," I said.

"Nothing like that. Well, kind of like that. I went to a club in New Jersey when I was in high school, that was a couple years before we moved here to be near my mama's sister. I learned to box in Jersey. I liked it okay, for exercise. Kept me in shape. Jumping rope, bag work. I won a lot of club fights."

"Pillow fights?"

"Oh, hell, Leonard," I said.

"No, it's all right. He's not wrong. I won on points a lot. I could keep from being hit by those guys, outpoint whoever

I fought, though I don't think I can outpoint you, Hap."

"On a good day, maybe," I said, "but you need to work on your striking power."

"I have. It isn't there."

"Least you know that," Leonard said. "Look, you got someone can move and hit, most of the time, they practice enough, they develop punching power, or more punching power, at least. But, Ty, I'm trying to save you some hurt here. You don't have it, and you ain't gonna have it. You're throwing picture-perfect punches, doing everything right, and the only way you're going to win a fight outside of points is wearing brass knuckles under your gloves, and they don't allow that."

Ty nodded. "Tell you another thing. My heart isn't in it. I don't want to be a boxer. I want the money to go to school."

"Like a college school?" Leonard asked.

"Like that, yeah. I've been interested in history for as long as I can remember. I think I'd like to teach it, or write books, or some such."

"Then go to college," I said.

"Can't afford it. I got a mother needs takin' care of. It's just me and her. She needs me to make some money, so I have to put college on hold. Bus saw me at the tennis courts, out there boxing with some friends, and he liked what he saw."

"You do look good," Leonard said, "but Bus, he sees a cleaning lady that can kick a mop bucket over, he might sign her. He uses boxers up and spits them out. White guy here today. Know him?"

"Not really. Met him couple times."

"Well, my guess is he sells these fights in some out-of-the-way place, and it's always some black kid against a white kid," Leonard said. "The great white hope, or some such shit, like it matters. Bus, he'll tell you how you're going to go big-time, jump to fighting big-time, make that big money, but he pushes too hard and too fast. And frankly, not only does he not give a shit about you, I don't think he knows talent when he sees it. Don't know or care you couldn't beat your way out of a wet paper bag."

"Don't sugarcoat it for him, Leonard."

"It's all right," Ty said. "Got in there with you today, Hap, and I could tell you were the first real fighter I'd been up against, way you moved, way you hit, caught me at angles. And I knew too, you were taking it easy on me. Thing is, they got me signed up and I need this fight, because I need the money. It's a big enough purse I can get Mama moved to a nicer place to live, and I can enroll for a semester."

"You got to win to spend it, Ty," Leonard said. "And say you did win, way Bus takes his cuts, well, it'll be less than promised. The towels are going to cost you, your space on that fucking bench, or wherever you sit before the fight that night, all goes on the tab. Fucking air you breathe, the sweat or blood you drop on the floor, the cleanup for it, that all goes on your tab. Even if you win it on points, then you got to go on to the next one, because that's the way it works. This white guy, the financier, he's just looking to see a black man get beaten by a white man. He probably made his mother pay him to suck her titty. You're in the water with sharks, Ty, and they are about to feast on your ass."

"They've promised me a certain amount, win or lose. So, I got to do it. All I can have you do is train me as best you can. I got a few days before the fight, and I have the athletic skills, just not the knockout skills. You say I can't get them, Leonard. But I have to believe I can."

"You can believe you can shit a sack of cat's-eye marbles, but it don't mean you can."

We drove to the tennis courts. We took some gloves with us. Wearing our regular clothes and shoes, we put the boxing gloves on him, and I put the other pair on Leonard.

"One thing Hap here showed me, out of Kenpo Karate, instead of always stepping and dragging the foot, leaving it in the bucket, he pushes off the back foot, which lunges him forward. That's how he's getting inside of you way he does. It has a lot of power too, because you got that train pushed from behind, not pulling the load forward. It ain't a boxer thing, but it's a real thing."

"Okay," Ty said. He was so earnest I wanted to hug him.

"I assume, Bus, bad a promoter and manager as he is,

has told you a few things. I know Dixie has. Dixie knows his stuff, by the way, but he's limited by the guy who pays him, that being Bus. He can only spend so much time, so he tries to give you the tools quick, same as us. They don't usually work when you get them wholesale. Understand that?"

Ty nodded.

"All right then. I'm going to move around with you a little, and we're going to do it slow, and Hap here, he's going to tell you the things you ought to know. Basic shit, and you're going to try and do them. Once we kind of got your warmed up, then me and you, we're going to go for it. I'm going to knock the shit out of you unless you cover up, do what's needed. I'll do it so you won't have brain damage, but I'm going to give you a taste of what you got coming."

"All right," Ty said.

"Hap," Leonard said. "Talk to him."

They started moving around, Leonard pawing light at him, the kid trying to outdance him. Leonard didn't have the footwork I had, and it wasn't as pretty as what the kid had, but Leonard didn't just move to move.

"Cover up," I said. "Flick his punches off by padding them, not just letting them hit the gloves solid, the arms solid. Punch catches you hard enough on the elbow, any part of your arms, if they guy is a thrower, you can get so you can't pick your arms up. Hard enough keeping them up during a fight when they're not hitting your arms, or you, so you can't just cover up and let your arms take a beating."

They moved around some more, and Leonard was cutting him off, slipping in closer. I kept talking.

"Thing I noticed when we were in the ring is you turn your head a lot, kind of narrow your eyes. Keep them open. Punches you see don't hit you more than the ones you do see, and psychologically, you see it coming, you can deal with it better if it does hit you."

"Really?" Ty said.

"He reads a lot of books," Leonard said, as they moved in a circle, pawing at each other lightly.

"Stay balanced. Don't stretch a punch too wide, because you do that, it won't have power and it'll get you off balance. You can get hit and knocked down just because you're off balance, but for them that don't know, it looks like a solid knockdown, and it sure as hell counts as one. Keep your feet under your shoulders, a little wider maybe, but not too wide.

"Here's a biggie. You got to hit back more often, and not just touch the opponent. Best way to keep your head on your shoulders is make him worry about his own. He throws something, you step back, or better yet, go sideways and inside and hit. Don't move your head right, then back to where it was, because that's how a combination finds you. Move your head when you need to, but don't just move it. You go from A to B, and back to A, you're going to get your brains scrambled.

"Jab, then a combination is good. But you don't need to jab to combine. Pad a shot off with your left, hit with the right, follow with hooks, uppercuts, whatever your guy is in position for. Know how to put a series of punches together, but know you got to sometimes put them together in different ways. And again, got your eyes open, you can pick your shots better. You got all that?"

"No."

"Sadly, that's just basic information, Ty. Now, here's what Leonard was telling you. You use your back foot like a springboard. Best to do this when he's in the process of throwing a punch, or it's about to arrive at the station. You got to get off the tracks and push in at the same time. Push off that back foot, which launches the front foot forward. Got to bring the back foot into position right away, not let it get stretched out. You got to push in so close you're damn near wearing his trunks, and I repeat, as you come in, you punch through him, not to him. All right. You two can start to boxing."

Leonard started off a little easy. The kid looked good, because he had that kind of body, but Leonard slipped him once and gave him an uppercut to the gut, and then doubled it up with a same-hand hook to Ty's jaw that sat him on his ass.

"You all right," Leonard said.

"Think so. That's the hardest I been hit."

"That's not good news," Leonard said. "That was my old-man-with-arthritis punch."

"Oh."

"Can you stand up?" I said.

"No."

"Sit there a moment, 'til you feel better."

We left him sitting there, and me and Leonard walked off to the side of the court and leaned against the high chain-link fence that bordered it.

Leonard said, "If he had six months to train, did it regularly, he'd still get knocked on his ass. He has one of those bodies, light as a feather when he moves, and heavy as a bag of cement when he hits the ground."

"Yeah. But on the positive side, you're getting that push-drag down."

"Yep. Look here, Hap. This guy, he wants to take care of his mother. I get that, but he'd better off working in the aluminum chair plant, saving up for about ten years."

"I don't think he'll go for that idea."

"Guy like that, ought to go to college, because he needs to stay away from things where he gets hit."

Ty was up by then, but he looked shaky.

He wandered our way.

"I can go again," Ty said.

"No, you can't," Leonard said. "I got a question for you."

Ty leaned against the fence next to me.

"So, this white guy, Mr. I Burned a Nigger Up," Leonard said. "He's seen you, all of us at the barn have, but the guy you're to box, his management, have they seen you?"

"First time I'll see them is the night of the bout."

"Yeah, well," Leonard said, "let me offer you an alternative to a cooling board in the funeral home."

Back at the barn, there was just us and Dixie. When we came in, Dixie was standing on the floor near the ring platform.

"Get dressed, Ty, we need to get cracking."

"We need to talk to you," Leonard said.

Ty wandered over to the far wall where there was a folding chair, and sat down in it. He looked at the floor.

"This guy," Leonard said. "We been working a little at the tennis courts. He could not get any older than he is now, be in the shape he's in, which is good, and train for six hundred years, and he couldn't knock a hole in a slice of Wonder Bread."

"And that might be an exaggeration of his punching power," I said.

"Yeah, well," Dixie said. "Figured as much. But you know, I just help train. I don't manage."

"That's a dodge, Dixie," Leonard said.

"Don't talk to me like that, you young pup."

"You mean don't tell you the truth," Leonard said. "That's what you mean."

"Maybe it is, but I'm in for the penny, so in for the pound."

126

"You're in for the money man," Leonard said. "You're in for that peckerwood with the sunglasses."

"All right. Guess I am."

"Ain't no guessing about it, Dixie. You're working for the man. You're the head field nigger, now, and you don't care what happens to the others long as you got your three squares and a cot."

"Goddamn you, Leonard. I ought to knock your block off."

"You ought to try."

For a moment, I thought Dixie might try.

"Guys," I said. "Bottom line, we don't need this to happen to Ty. Way me and Leonard see it, the guy he's supposed to be fighting, his management, they don't know Ty from a hole in the ground."

"Different fighter shows up," Leonard said, "they're none the wiser."

"Ah, but Bus knows," Dixie said. "Money man, he knows."

"Don't matter," Leonard said. "I show up ready to fight, they got to let me go in, or forfeit the match. Whatever way it turns out, Ty doesn't end up with his brains scrambled, and if money is won, he gets it. Shit, Dixie, he's professor material, not boxing material."

"They won't like I'm in on that," Dixie said.

"No, they won't. But you can be that head field nigger, or you can help Ty out."

Dixie took a deep breath. He turned his head and

watched the light come through the beating slats of the swamp cooler.

"All right," he said.

Fight night was a rainy night, and the place where the fight was held was deep in the woods on a huge concrete slab inside a big aluminum building that had all the architectural class of a boxcar.

A man just inside, tall and white and bald, was taking money for seats. There were bleachers on three sides of the ring, and one side had fold-out aluminum chairs. There was a section of bleachers for black attendees and the rest were for the whites, except for the fold-out chairs that were for the fighters and their managers and trainers and the like.

The ring in the center of the place was lower than the ring in the barn, and there were lights set up everywhere, and it would have been hot in there except for the big fan in the ceiling that was beating the air around.

The white man who had been with Bus was with Bus again. When we came in, Leonard wearing a pink bathrobe got a big laugh from the crowd.

The white man came over with Bus, and they looked at us, then they turned their attention to Dixie.

"What's he doing here?" the white man said.

"Why, he's going to knock your boy out," Dixie said.

"What the hell, Dixie?" Bus said.

"Ty has a replacement tonight," Leonard said. "Me."

"Where's Ty?" Bus said.

"Home reading a book, I figure," Leonard said.

"It's supposed to be him, not you," the white man said. "I didn't make any agreement with you."

"You got one now. I'm fighting for Ty, and no one but you folks know me here, so I'm as good as being Ty as not. I'm also a better fighter. That worry you?"

"Not in the least," the white man said.

"You can cancel, you want," Leonard said.

"Okay, smart guy. Have it your way. You'll wish you stayed home in about thirty minutes or so."

Bus said, "You in on this, Dixie?"

"Might as well be."

"You and me are done."

"No. I quit first, soon as this fight is over, no matter what the outcome."

"I hope Hedge beats your brains out," the white guy said, "but I don't figure you have any to begin with."

"Maybe," Leonard said. "But I got a big dick."

The white man walked away practically with a rain cloud hovering over his head. He crossed in front of the ring and went through a door on the far side. I got a glimpse of light from in the room there before he closed the door.

"He doesn't like you," I said to Leonard.

"I don't like you or him," Bus said. "And Dixie, I

wouldn't have thought this of you."

"That's what worries me," Dixie said. "You had me all laid out in your mind. Ty could have been killed. He couldn't hold his own with either of these boys, and you didn't care long as he looked like he could fight, and you got paid."

"It's a business," Bus said.

"Yeah," Dixie said. "So was the slave trade. Thing is, though, Leonard here, he's our fighter tonight, so accept it."

"What's with the fucking pink bathrobe?" Bus said.

"A tip," Leonard said. "Don't wash your whites with your reds."

"Goddamn you fuckers," Bus said, and walked over to one of the folding chairs near the ring and sat down.

"He's pissed," I said.

"Think so?" Leonard said. "I thought he seemed all right."

"He don't matter no more," Dixie said.

"One thing," Leonard said. "You're going to be in my corner, Dixie, but I want Hap there too."

"Doing what? Holding your hand?"

"If it comes to it."

There was some commotion across the way, and the door on the far side opened wide and the white man came back in, and now he had two others with him. A chubby white guy wearing a T-shirt and loose pants and tennis shoes, and a beer truck of a man that had on a white sweat-shirt with a white hood. Under the hood was a white face and eyes as blue and cold as glacial ice.

Their boxer was wide across the shoulders, thick in the chest, at least six-four, with legs like the trunks of trees, massive feet and hands. His chin was as solid-looking as a cement block, and the ridge of bone over his eyes was thick. His ears looked like cauliflowers and his nose was flat. He smiled at us. He had a missing upper front tooth.

"Man, that's a face only his dog could love," I said.

"Damn," Dixie said. "Makes Man Slayer look like a yard gnome. It's not too late for an early retirement, Leonard."

"I'm all right," Leonard said, but the words took time to arrive.

They pulled wooden steps from under the ring platform on both sides, as well as stools. The steps were pushed against the ring, and the stools were put inside the ring.

Leonard and the walking mountain went up their steps and stood in their corners, neither bothering with the stools. The white crowd called Leonard everything but a human. He just grinned at them.

The black crowd cheered for Leonard. The white crowd cheered for the mountain. A theme had developed.

I came up the steps after Dixie and stood next to Leonard in his corner.

Leonard said, "This does not look good."

"No, sir," I said. "It does not."

"Before things get started," Dixie said, "you could say you got to go pee, and just not come back."

"I'm all right," Leonard said.

"Well yeah," I said. "For right now."

A stocky white man with a crew cut, wearing a white shirt and black pants, climbed into the ring carrying a megaphone. He looked out over the rambunctious, loud crowd.

"Cut it out!" he called into the megaphone. He had to repeat that a couple of times, but the crowd finally settled down.

"Tonight, I'm the referee, Tom Ray. We got ten rounds of boxing. And boxing it will be, and the crowd will maintain itself. White folks will watch and enjoy. Colored folks will watch and enjoy. I don't want trouble. In this corner," he pointed to the big man, "is James Hedge." He then pointed to Leonard, and called out Ty's name. He ended with, "Now, let's get on with this event."

Leonard and the mountain moved to the center of the ring and got instructions from the referee. While the ref talked, they were glaring at one another. If someone had crossed their line of vision, I wouldn't have been surprised if they had burst into fire.

They went to their corners, and neither he nor Leonard sat on their stools. They stood and rubbed their shoes in some resin that had been put there for just that.

Leonard said, "I got this guy."

"Of course, you do," I said.

"What is he, thirty years old?"

"He's twenty-four," Dixie said. "Twenty-four hard fucking years. Five in prison. Before that, a bit of reform school. Trust me, don't put your guard down."

"I'll have my hands up plenty, and they'll be hitting him."

"That's right," I said.

"Don't get cocky," Dixie said.

"You know of any weak spots he's got?" Leonard asked.

"He gets tired around round nine."

"That's a weak spot? That's damn near the whole fight."

"Sorry, Leonard," Dixie said.

The mountain's cornerman was standing behind him, rubbing his shoulders. After a moment, he stopped and pulled the stool and himself through the ropes, stood on the edge of the platform. Me and Dixie did the same.

A guy on the side of the ring hit a piece of angle iron with a short piece of pipe, and that served as the bell. We were into round one.

Leonard was strong for his age, and pretty damn quick, but when Leonard hit Hedge it was like hitting a six-foot-four fireplug. The guy's defense was his face, which seemed hard to hurt.

I tell you true as the night is dark, Leonard was hitting Hedge so hard a bull would have gone to its knees and begged for mercy. But this guy, he just kept coming, didn't move his head at all.

Leonard hit Hedge over the eyes with a series of jabs, kind of shots that normally bring blood, but this guy, the ridge over his eyes was hard and scarred and didn't seem to have any blood in it.

First round was mostly Hedge inching forward and Leonard hitting him with jabs and a couple of crosses that were picture-perfect. When he hit Hedge, the sweat came off Hedge's face and sprayed up into the light and made a kind of golden mist. Toward the end of the round Hedge caught Leonard in the ribs with a couple of hooks that probably gave Leonard's childhood teddy bear consternation.

When the bell rang, Leonard came back to the corner and sat on his stool this time. The muscles in his back were jumping a little, and Dixie went into rubbing him down.

"You think I hurt him any?" Leonard said to me.

"Nope."

"Aren't you supposed to encourage me?"

"Well, he hasn't really hit you good yet."

"He hit my ribs pretty good, my left elbow. He's slow, but when he lands one it's like a sledgehammer."

"I think you got to stay away from his head a little more, work his body. Frankly, you get a chance to rabbit punch him or slip one into his balls, you might want to do it. Something needs to make him tire a little. Look at him."

He was sitting on a stool, looking like he felt good enough to take time to read a magazine—if he could read.

"I got this," Leonard said.

"So you say."

"Yeah, I might ought to catch him one in the balls."

Bell clanged and Leonard went back out there, coming to the center of the ring first. He gave Hedge a series of jabs to the head, and then started slamming hooks to the body. They didn't seem to be doing any more harm than the jabs.

They clenched a couple of times, and once or twice Leonard hit him in the back of the head, and got separated by the referee and got a warning.

Leonard didn't take the warning to heart. Next time in he swung an uppercut to Hedge's stomach, then another to his balls.

It was solid, and the referee stepped in, and Hedge said, "Nah, it's all right."

Leonard said it was an accident, which it wasn't, and they went at it again.

Hedge took a series of jabs, and then he swung a hard hook. Leonard put his arm up, but this one was a really good one, and hit Leonard's arm and slipped off the sweat and caught Leonard over the left ear and knocked him down.

I was wishing he'd stay down, but I knew better than that. Not while there was life in him. Leonard got up on the count of four.

"I slipped," he said.

"Yeah, after he knocked your black ass down," said the referee.

Leonard rode the bicycle for the rest of the round, the white crowd booing, and even some of the black crowd.

When the bell rang and Leonard came back to his stool, he said, "He's going to kill me."

"What I was thinking."

Dixie gave Leonard a sip of water and Leonard spat it into a bucket.

"You can box him all day long, and you might even get some points," Dixie said, "but these motherfuckers don't count points. They count knockouts and dead."

"Your suggestion for me is what?" Leonard said.

"Don't get hit."

"That's it?"

"Listen, you got to tie him up a couple of rounds, let him wear down."

"I'm the one wearing down."

"Dance with him, then grab him and get in close. Step on his foot, and soon as you do, uppercut him to the chin, hard as you can. Not on the point, like you hear, but just behind that, so you don't break your goddamn hand. It'll do the same thing as a tip-of–the-chin shot. Side of the jaw is even better than that."

"All right."

"But mostly, don't get hit."

"You finish up here tonight, Dixie, you ought to maybe be like a motivational speaker," Leonard said.

The bell rang, and Leonard went back out.

Well, there was dancing for a while, and then damn if Leonard didn't hit Hedge so hard with a hook to the face, the force of it knocked Leonard off balance and he fell down.

The white crowd went wild for a moment.

The referee did call that one a slip.

The white crowd booed. The black crowd cheered.

I studied Hedge. He looked calm and dumb, like he was thinking about something less than profound. Like why do dogs like bones? If he was any calmer, they could let him fight from an easy chair in front of the TV.

Leonard was shuffling a lot, dancing still. Getting in close hadn't worked as well for him as he had hoped, so he was back on his bicycle. He was really starting to sweat.

The bell rang.

Back on the stool, Dixie worked on Leonard's legs. The muscles and nerves in them were jumping like frogs

"You okay?" I said.

"He hasn't really nailed me but a couple of times, but those times worry me some. There might be more of them."

"That one you hit him with when you were in close," Dixie said. "That hurt him."

"Think so?" Leonard said. "I didn't notice."

"He actually blinked once or twice," Dixie said.

"Probably had something in his eye," Leonard said.

"His legs bent a little," Dixie said. "Not much, but a little. A little ain't much, but it's something."

"You notice that, Hap? Me making him sag a little?"

"No," I said.

"Telling you, you hurt him," Dixie said. "You need to do it again."

The bell rang, and Leonard went back out. He gave Hedge a series of blows, and I mean they were good ones. Anyone else had taken shots like that, they'd be in a padded room trying to figure out how to sort white socks by colors.

But Hedge, he didn't seem to notice. It went on like this for a couple more rounds.

Back in the corner, Dixie said, "You want me to stop it?"

"Hell no . . . Well, not yet," Leonard said. "Hap, you got a blow gun, maybe you could shoot that motherfucker with a poison dart."

"Get back inside of him," Dixie said. "Listen to me, and you might get to go home and not in a box. You might survive, anyway. But you got to get in there and do what I'm telling you. Close in, and work those uppercuts."

"All right, Dixie. Bury me in blue, please. Hap, put my cowboy hat on my chest. The one with the chin string."

Bell rang. Leonard went out again.

It was as before for about half the round, and then I noticed when Leonard tied Hedge up, got those uppercuts in, as Dixie said, Hedge was buckling a little. Very little, but his knees bent and even wobbled slightly. Weren't watching for it, it didn't seem like much, but I was watching hard. Hedge was blinking too, like he was trying to find focus.

Dixie knew his stuff.

When the bell rang, Hedge went back to his corner more slowly than before. Leonard sat on his stool like a sack of potatoes.

"You got him," Dixie said.

"I'm what you might call uncertain."

"You don't get hit solid in the next round, he'll go," Dixie said.

"You base this on what?"

"I saw it too, Leonard. It's those uppercuts under the chin that he doesn't wear too well."

"That's right," Dixie said. "You got to tie him up more."

"He's stronger than me," Leonard said.

"Yeah, but he isn't hitting you much."

"Funny, I feel like he is."

"He's not," I said. "Not like you're hitting him."

The bell rang and out Leonard went. As he neared Hedge, Hedge threw a lazy left hook that Leonard ducked under, but then a right hook caught him and knocked Leonard on his ass. Leonard lay back on the canvas, looked at the ceiling lights.

Leonard slowly rolled on his side and got his hands under him and got up at an eight count. He tried to dance a little after that, but he didn't have much dancing left in him. Now it was toe-to-toe, and Leonard got in some damn good hooks to the ribs. Those hooks were having serious effect now. Hedge started dropping his elbows to cover his ribs, and then Leonard started jabbing him, and I could tell those jabs were beginning to work too, due to plain old attrition.

Leonard got inside of him, tied him up. Hedge slung him around a bit, but Leonard got an uppercut in, and it was solid. You could hear it all over the place, like someone had dropped a bag of dry concrete.

Leonard had begun to chip off Hedge's armor. He got inside again and tied Hedge up, slipped a double uppercut with the right in. Hedge sort of bounced back on his heels, stumbled, righted himself, then fell back again, against the ropes.

Leonard skipped in and started hooking Hedge to the head, one shot after another. Then he zipped an uppercut in, caught Hedge just under the chin, and Hedge did that little hop again, hit the ropes, bounced forward, and Leonard threw a right cross at him that was loaded with everything but the kitchen sink and a blacksmith's anvil.

Hedge fell backwards, stiff as a board, hit the ropes, rolled off them, landed facedown on the floor with a smack, spit his mouthpiece out, and passed a little fluttering fart that sounded like a weak blast on a kazoo.

"Knocked him right into the shit house," Dixie said.

Leonard returned to his corner. The referee started counting, and when he got to nine, I knew there wasn't any way Hedge was going to get up short of a winch and a pully.

"And the winner," the referee said, and called Ty's name, which, of course, was Leonard.

Leonard lumbered to the center of the ring and the referee lifted his hand and held it up.

There were yells from the white crowd, and cheers from the black crowd, and Leonard said, "I need me a steak and a jug of ice tea, and a goddamn big-ass bowl of banana pudding with vanilla wafers in it."

"Come on, let's get a move on," Dixie said.

When we climbed out of the ring, Bus came over. "You did it, Leonard."

"My name is Ty," Leonard said. "It's better for all of us you don't forget that."

"So it is," Bus said.

"What about the prize money?" I said.

"Come by and get it tomorrow, at the barn. Three o'clock."

"Don't try and play me none now," Leonard said. "I can do to you what I did to him."

"Don't get too proud of yourself," Bus said. "You had some luck."

"No," Dixie said. "Luck had nothing to do with it."

Leonard didn't have a steak or banana pudding. When we came out, it was raining and the white crowd was aggressive and the black crowd was pushing back at them.

I thought it might all go to hell, but the referee came out and pulled a pistol from under his rain slicker and fired a shot in the air.

"Now back off," the ref said. "Nigger won fair and square."

"He's just the sweetest," Leonard said.

We got in the car and Dixie drove us out of there.

Leonard ended up staying at Dixie's. I stayed there too. Leonard hurt too much to eat. His jaws couldn't have worked over a spoonful of tapioca pudding. He was asleep on Dixie's couch in an instant. I unbuttoned his boxing shoes and slipped them off; Dixie covered him with a blanket.

At the kitchen table, Dixie said, "I'm going to be moving. What about you and Leonard?"

"We'll play it out."

"Good luck on that. Want coffee?"

I didn't know what I wanted, but I said, "Yes."

Dixie made coffee and we sat at the table and sipped it.

"Leonard would make a hell of a boxer," Dixie said. "Could go all the way. And you too, except you got a streak of kindness in you."

"Just a streak," I said. "Look, you really think you got to run from all this?"

"I'm thinking that. Yeah."

"Me and Leonard, we'll get the money for Ty tomorrow. You don't need to be there."

Dixie was silent for a time. He sipped his coffee.

"Yeah. I need to be there. You might want to call Ty, tell him he won."

Ty didn't go with us the next day, partly because he was embarrassed, and mostly because we asked him not to.

"There's no point to it," Leonard said. "You're there, they're going to be mad at you more than us. And by the way, you been in that ring other night, you'd be dead, or close enough to it they'd have the food tube down your throat."

So we left him home, bought Leonard a Dairy Queen vanilla cone, and drove out to the barn. When we walked in, it was sticky hot and the fan wasn't on, and there was no wind moving through the open windows or the gaps in the swamp cooler. Just dead air, heavy as disappointment.

Dixie, Bus, Hedge, and that asshole white-guy promoter were all standing at the bottom of the platform that held the boxing ring.

Hedge had taken Leonard's shots without much blood, but on this day, he looked a lot worse than Leonard, who was wearing Band-Aids like a fashion statement, and had a bit of a hitch in his get-along.

In contrast, Hedge's face was swollen and could have been mistaken for a volleyball with bits of hair on it. I got the impression he had been too sore to shave. His eyes were narrow due to that swelling, and his shoulders were slumped. He gave the impression he was ready for a trip to the garbage dump and willing to be shot dead before he got the ride.

When we got close to them, the white promoter stepped out, said, "I guess you've come for the other nigger's money. You ain't getting it."

I said, "Why not?"

"You cheated. You put in a ringer."

"You cheated, your guy is a ringer and Bus here knew Ty would wind up in the cabbage bin at the Piggly Wiggly, and he didn't care."

"I didn't know any such thing," Bus said.

"Yeah, you did," Dixie said.

"I thought I told you, you were through."

"You did, but I'm here today, gone tomorrow."

"You could end up gone for a long time," said the white promoter. "Look here. I got the money your monkey won, but it was the wrong monkey."

"You let the fight go on," I said. "Had Leonard lost, you'd be expecting some dough. Way I have it figured, you and Bus are like Siamese twins. You had your bets on one guy, Hedge here."

"You broke the rules," the promoter said.

"So did you, planning on throwing some showboat who couldn't fight into the path of this semitruck," I said. "Leonard here just happened to be better. Hedge, they don't care about you. They put you out there until you can't be out anymore, then they get a new semitruck."

Hedge didn't say anything.

"Well," the promoter said, "however you see it, you aren't getting the money. Hedge here gets his cut, and me and Bus take ours, but your monkey has to buy his own bananas with his own money."

"Call me a monkey one more time," Leonard said. "Please do."

"I think he's talking about Ty," Bus said.

"Ah," Leonard said. "That makes it all right, don't it? So, let me rephrase it. Call anyone a monkey, I'll fix your little red wagon good."

The promoter might have considered saying something, but he didn't. He just took a deep breath.

"Give 'em the money," Hedge said.

"What?" the promoter said.

"You heard me. Man here beat me fair and square."

"You ain't listening here," the promoter said. "They didn't play fair."

"Didn't you tell me to try and kill this fella?" Hedge said.

"Symbolically," the promoter said.

"Give him the money."

"I'm not—"

He didn't get another word out. Hedge swiveled and hit him square in the face with a nasty left hook, and the promoter fell back against the ring and then onto the floor.

"Damn," Leonard said. "I remember those hooks. One more round of those and I'd have lost."

"You know that's right," Hedge said, bent down and looked through the promoter's coat pockets, came out with a stash of cash. When he stood up, he had a folded wad of money with a rubber band around it.

Hedge said, "I got some coming for being in the fight. The rest of it, you can do with what you want. You earned it."

Hedge removed the rubber band and slowly peeled off what he was owed, wetting his thumb and finger between bills until he had his share.

He handed Leonard the rest of the money.

"I'm going to go home, have some coffee, fuck the wife, then go see if I can get on at the foundry in Tyler. Boxing is tiring and the pay sucks."

"Good luck," I said.

"Same to you, kid." Hedge reached out and gently touched Leonard on the shoulder. "I never fought nobody harder and never been fought as hard. Couple years on you, and you'll be hard to beat even with a pipe wrench."

"I know that," Leonard said.

"He knows it," I said.

Hedge laughed and walked away and was quickly out of the barn and gone.

Leonard said, "What's your share, Dixie?"

"Keep my share. Ty will need it."

"All right," Leonard said.

"I got a cut coming," Bus said.

"No," I said. "No, you don't."

"This won't go over well with me and some other folks," Bus said.

"Woo, the spooky I-got-assholes-in-high-places card," Leonard said.

"Gonna be what it's gonna be, Bus," Dixie said. "And part of what it's going to be is you ain't getting paid."

"You were a part of it," Bus said.

"Yeah, I lied to myself a lot. But I'm done quit with that. I fucking resign big-time, and you can kiss my black ass bye-bye on my way out the door."

We went to Ty's house and gave him the money and met his mother, who was a nice lady with faded clothes that smelled faintly of laundry soap and starch. She gave us each a slice of buttermilk pie and a glass of milk.

We sat at the table and ate. After we talked about how Ty was going to college, how he would do great things, his mother cried a little.

Later, me and Leonard and Ty went out in the yard and

stood by my car. It was a bleak spot where Ty was living. We could see the smoke from burning garbage at the city dump.

"I can't believe you did this for me," Ty said.

"Me either," Leonard said, touching one of the Band-Aids on his head.

"I feel like a fraud."

"You are," I said, "but it's good that you are, or you'd be busted up something awful."

"I know that's right," Ty said.

"Damn straight," Leonard said. "Listen here. Bus was the fraud. He fed you some shit about your skills. He knew you looked pretty but hit soft. Or he didn't care enough one way or the other, however you want to look at it. But here's the thing. I was made for battle and you were made for the books. You go on and do good with yourself."

"Will the promoter and Bus be coming after you fellows?"

"I don't think so," I said. "I think the promoter was a blowhard and wanted people to think he was tough. I think Bus might pack up a grip and move on."

"Thinking the same," Leonard said.

"I guess we'll be leaving soon," Ty said.

"Just in case I'm wrong about how the losers feel and what they can do, I'd suggest it, and right away," Leonard said.

We shook hands with Ty, and got in the car.

I said, "You really think the losers are done with us?"

"I think so. We might want to be cautious for a while, but I think so."

We drove away, and by the time we did that it was close to noon. I drove us to the café and parked in front of it.

Leonard said, "What are you doing?"

"I don't know about you, but that pie was like an appetizer. I'm still tired from watching you take a beating and give one, and I'm thinking I need a good meal to boost back my energy."

"You ought to be on this end. But I thought you didn't want to have me go in a café like this with you. A white café."

"Like you said, there's a law now. Besides, we've done been in there and you gave your opinions on breakfast items, and I'm thinking about the lunch special. Saw it on the menu. Beans and greens, or you can go for chicken and dumplings and greens. That's the way I'll go. Shit, man. I might even get another piece of pie of some kind. They might have chocolate meringue. Some coffee would be nice too."

"I ain't having none of that pie they use whip cream on the top and not meringue, I'll tell you that."

"You're saying about something you don't even know is a fact."

"I like to be prepared for disappointment. Fact is, screw chocolate pie, meringue, whip cream, or dog sput. I'd like some banana pudding—they got that and they put actual vanilla wafers in it, I'll be all over it like a duck on a fucking June bug."

"What's with you and vanilla wafers, vanilla ice cream, cookies and such?"

"I like vanilla."

"Fair enough. Shall we go in?"

"With bells on. Just let me shift five or ten pounds of my balls to the left, where I feel the most comfortable, and I'm ready."

We got out of the car, and Leonard, splotched with Band-Aids, went up the walk with a skipping motion, and moved ahead of me through the door into the café.

THE SABINE WAS HIGH

"Home from the war, home from the seas,
out of the skies, and weak in the knees."
—Jersey Fitzgerald

I HAD GOTTEN A PHONE CALL from Leonard a few days before he was to be mustered out, and he told me where he would be coming in, told me he wanted me to pick him up at the bus station in Tyler. From there, he wanted to go camping and fishing.

It was raining that day, and the water ran across the highway in silver sheets and filled the ditches on either side of it. The Sabine River actually touched the sides of the high bridge's upper railing, and the water sloshed onto the highway.

I tooled on into Tyler, over to the bus station. The old colored section was still there, and most of the black people were sitting there, even though legally they didn't have to.

I looked at the clock on the wall. I was early. I went to the coffee machine, dropped a few coins in. The cup came out upside down and the coffee hit the bottom of the cup and sprayed out onto me. The coffee was the color of diarrhea.

I tried again, and the cup was right this time, but the coffee tasted like what it looked like. I threw it in the trash and bought a package of peanut butter crackers, but the crackers were stale, and the peanut butter had a nasty taste somewhere between river mud and brick mortar. I tossed the crackers too.

I went outside. The rain had stopped. I walked out to my car and sat in it, read from a book I had in the glove box. I always had a book. It was science fiction. But I wasn't in a mood to read. I walked back to the station. I looked at my watch, but I wasn't wearing it. Inside the station I glanced at the clock again. It was five minutes until arrival time.

At the ticket desk I asked if the bus was on time.

The fat man behind the counter, who looked as if he had been built by stacking snowballs in three piles like Frosty the Snowman, and may have bought his clothes from a clown store, said, "We'll know if they show up on time, won't we?"

This was impossible to argue with. I thanked him and went back outside. I leaned on the wall. I saw there were flies on the wall next to me, high up close to the roof. I guess they were having a picnic, or maybe just a family reunion. I watched them for a while, and then I watched the road in front of the bus station.

The Greyhound came rolling in, shiny from the rain. The hound design on the side of the bus looked happy and in a hurry. The bus brakes hissed and the bus bumped a little as it stopped.

The bus door whispered open, and people started out. The first one out was a tall, well-constructed woman in her thirties wearing a blue miniskirt and blue top with the confidence of a nun who thinks being a bride to Christ means she'll someday get epic action from Jesus. She had on white boots, and her brown hair was piled at the top but long in back. Watching her walk into the station, I almost forgot I was there for Leonard.

Looking back at the bus, I saw Leonard get off. The sunlight made his black skin shine. I guess I was expecting him to be in uniform for some reason, but he wasn't. He was wearing blue jeans and cowboy boots and a blue western shirt with a blue jean jacket. He had a brown cowboy hat in his hand and a duffel bag slung across his back on a strap. He looked at me and smiled.

There are some people you don't talk to for a couple years, maybe more, and soon as you see them, it's like they have only left the room for a moment, and that's how it was with me and Leonard.

In the car, we chatted about this and that, nothing special. We hadn't gone far before we stopped at a Brookshire's store, bought some food and drinks for the fishing trip.

We bought some lard and hot dogs, a carton of eggs that we well-padded with paper bags, and put them in a Styrofoam cooler, along with some Dr Peppers and some Budweiser, bought some chips and buns, a few assorted items, along with a couple boxes of vanilla wafers. We packed them and the cooler in the back seat of the car. I had rods and reels and fishing tackle in the trunk, along with a folded tent and some other camping goods.

"So, how was it over there?" I said.

"Wet like this, but a lot more of the time, and maybe wetter. Definitely wetter. You walked through the jungle after a rain, the foliage steamed when the sun came out and there were more snakes and insects there than here, and there were these folks in black pajamas who wanted to kill you with guns. They made booby traps too. Pits with spikes coated in dung down at the bottom. Fell on one of those, spike didn't kill you, the infection would. The Cong were tough. It was dark in the jungle, sometimes even when the sun was high, and at other times you went along trails where the moon was so full and bright, you could see in front of you better than if you had a flashlight. The enemy killed friends of mine, and I killed the enemy when I could. I did my duty, Hap, and I'd do it again, I was asked to. That's how it was in a nutshell."

"I did my duty too, Leonard."

"Yeah. I know. How was prison?"

"Not as damp as the jungle, but it's a jungle of its own, concrete and bars and people who got nothing to gain or lose by sticking a knife in your gut, saying they just wanted to rid the world of cowards who wouldn't fight a war. I had to adjust their thinking a little from time to time. I only got stabbed twice. Minor stuff."

"So, like me, you had it pretty easy?"

"I wouldn't have traded with you."

"You know, I wouldn't have traded with you. I don't know I could handle prison, even a short term. Hey, you know what's good?"

"What?"

"You get a big glass mug, and you put it in the freezer section of the refrigerator until it frosts over, and then you pour it three-quarters full of Dr Pepper, and top it off with vanilla ice cream. Don't let it set long, just drink it right away, and it's like a gift from the gods."

"Which gods?"

"Whichever ones I want to make up in the moment."

"We didn't buy any ice cream."

"I'm just saying it's good. We don't have any frosted mugs either, but I'm telling you, try it, it's so damn tasty, while you're drinking it, you could jack off with a hand full of briars and feel nothing but that cool drink and that ice cream sliding down your throat."

We nearly drove all the way back to Marvel Creek, but just before, took a road into the Sabine River bottoms. It was a gravel road, and it went by a place where the woods had been cleared and there was a big building and some concrete slabs. They used to hold illegal fights there. Once, Leonard had boxed against a behemoth named Hedge, and Leonard beat him, but it was close.

I drove us to a place near the river where the woods had been beat back and there was a concrete picnic table under some trees. A square of fire-stained bricks with a metal grate over it had been put near it for cooking. Table and cooker had been there for years. No one knew who built either. There were beer cans scattered about. Over the river you could see an old rickety metal bridge supported by cables and rust. Soon the bridge, like a lot of my plans, would fall into the Sabine and be carried away.

I parked, and the first thing we did was pick up all the beer cans. We put them in a tow sack I kept in the trunk of the car for this and that, and then we tied the bag off and set it in the back seat of the car.

We decided to pitch our tent over the picnic table, so we'd have it inside. It was the perfect campsite.

When the tent was pitched, we were covered with sweat. Now that the rain had passed, the air had become humid, and it stuck to us like Brer Rabbit Syrup.

Going through the fishing tackle, we found what we wanted and got our hooks set, pulled a couple of folded lawn chairs out of the trunk and took them and the rods down to the edge of the water.

We unfolded the chairs and sat and cast into the muddy Sabine, which was rolling along high and furious, rushing its water toward the Gulf of Mexico.

We weren't using live bait, just the stuff from the fishing tackle box, the false flies and so on. Neither of us were particularly good fishermen, but we had discovered long ago that we liked to sit and anticipate. We had rods, but we often used the old standby, cane poles. Fishing gave us something to do that didn't really matter. If we caught fish, I had the fry pan and the stuff to cook them; if we didn't, there were the hot dogs.

A big water moccasin swam by in the center of the river, either caught up by the churning water or on his way down deep south for a snake fiesta.

"Big motherfucker," Leonard said.

"You should see his brother."

"You don't know he's got a brother."

"You don't know he doesn't. He might have a sister."

That was our way, stupid jokes and companionship. There were moments when we didn't need anything other than that.

Leonard said, "When's the last time we did this?"

"I don't know. Been a while."

Leonard breathed deep, let out a sigh.

"One time, over there, long before I was back in the world, I saw a Vietnamese, little guy, riding a bicycle. He wasn't a soldier, or at least he didn't seem to be, but he was in the wrong place at the wrong time. We were on a hill and we could see him in the distance, riding along next to a huge stretch of jungle. Our jets were flying overhead, coming down close to the tops of the trees because it was thought the Cong were in that piece of forest, hiding, and that's where our squad was going. The lieutenant, to make it safer for us, called in a napalm strike. Nasty stuff, dropped out of the jets in a thick, fiery goo.

"I'm watching this guy, and he's pedaling fast. Hears the planes, looks up, pedals faster, thinking maybe he could outrun them or some such stupid thought, and out comes that dark burning mess from a couple of jets, and it falls fast and hits him the way it hits the jungle, and zap, the jungle disappears in a roar of flame and this crackle like dry leaves underfoot, but way louder, and the bicycle guy, he disappears too. Just plain ceased to be. He wasn't boiled. Wasn't set on fire. He was gone, Hap. And you know what? I thought it was funny as hell. We all laughed. Just some poor guy riding along on his bicycle, and the next thing you know his village is looking for him. You know, hey, anybody seen Bob? Wasn't he supposed to bring some rice home for supper? They not only weren't going to find him, they weren't going to find his bicycle either. I mean that shit disintegrated him and his bike, like pouring salt on a slug, but a faster process. I laughed, Hap. Funniest thing I had seen in months, just hysterical. I didn't think about his family, probably never knowing what happened to him, or why. I just thought it was funny, so funny, I cried. I still think about it, and now, when I wake up thinking about it, I don't find it so funny."

"Release valve, Leonard. Fireman, policeman, the military, they all do it. Probably emergency room folks as well. Sometimes, you got to laugh to keep from crying. Prison could be like that."

"I don't know I felt that way, though, Hap. I got so if their eyes were slanted, I hated them all. I don't have any regrets fighting for our country, but I sometimes got to wonder where the line really was, you know, and I got to think too how it changed me for a time, maybe forever, and I'm not sure I got enough excuses to make me comfortable about it."

"Why I didn't go, Leonard. No war is good or pretty, but that stuff with Hitler, I'm pretty sure had I been around then, I would have got into that. Vietnam. Different thing. Political war over unclear politics. The line was firmer between us and them in World War Two. Guarantee you, no matter what flag they fly under, won't be long when they'll be as capitalistic as us, and we'll be visiting them for vacations, and because of the money, they'll be glad to see us."

"I suppose. But I did what I thought was right."

"But it may not have been right."

"Could be, Hap. Could be."

We cranked in our false bait and cast again, but with the water the way it was, it just carried our lines, and it was all we could do not to tangle them together or mix them into the debris of limbs and leaves that were washing by.

"One time, in prison, I'm in one of the many lines we had to make to do this or that, and we were so close you damn near got your dick in the guy's ass in front of you—"

"Maybe I did make the wrong choice."

"I think you might have found the company less than romantic, Leonard."

"Didn't say anything about feeling romantic."

"So, I'm in a line, and this guy, he breaks the line, and he's got this little sticker, shank, whatever you want to call it, though I never hear anyone say shank when I was in prison. He comes up to this one guy in line and reaches out quick with his free hand and wraps his arm around the guy and pushes the knife into him, uses his body like he's fucking, you know, pushing it against the knife, back and forth, did that fast as a bunny gets pussy. This other guy in line was in on it, you know. He grabs the poor guy from behind and helps hold him so he won't fall, and this other con keeps knife-fucking him until there's blood all over the floor. Usually, something like that, they stab quick and they're gone. But these guys, they were in for life and didn't give a shit. They didn't stop until the guy was dead. It happened fast, but there was a part of me that thought I should help. But the guy they killed, he was no peach either, but still, I felt helpless and guilty for not at least trying to stop them. The guy getting stabbed, he turned his head toward me once, like he was asking for help, and I didn't do anything. No one did. It was over pretty damn fast.

"Found out later the beef was over one of them feeling he had been insulted by that guy, but no one remembered the insult. Think about that, Leonard. They killed him in a horrible way over one of them thinking he was insulted, yet he couldn't remember the insult. And here's the corker, guy did the stabbing. Guards figured out what was what pretty quick. They took him away, put him in the hole, and then for whatever reason, they let him out a few months later. He and his buddy, one who had held that guy while the stabbing was done, they got into some altercation over a chocolate bar. The stabber wanted to eat it, and the erstwhile assistant to the murder, he was saving it to melt so he could grease up a convict's asshole for fucking. Guy who had helped the stabber kill that guy over an insult, was stabbed by his friend who just got out of the hole. Where the fuck did he get a tool that quick? Why did they let him out of solitary confinement after what he did, just drop him back into the prison population, this guy from hell? Right then, I understood the death penalty, at least for a select few, and I've never had a moral question about it since for creatures like that.

"Anyway, the stabber got taken away this time, put in the hole again, and a few days in, he decided to beat his brains out on the wall rather than be there. He succeeded. Can you imagine that type of determination?"

"I think he was a good judge of character," Leonard said.

"Let me tell you something. Soon as I heard he beat his brains out on a concrete wall, I laughed. Funniest goddamn thing I could imagine. It wasn't just me, the guards and the prisoners heard about it, they thought it was hysterical. One of the guards said, 'So he beat his head on the wall and all that came out was oatmeal, no brains,' and at the time that seemed damn funny, and it's just silly."

"Makes me laugh a little," Leonard said.

We quit talking. It was quiet for a while, except for the sound of the river rushing along. We kept reeling in our line and recasting. After an hour of this, Leonard said, "I think we need some different bait."

"Maybe," I said.

We didn't get up to dig for worms, and we were too far away from a good spot for grasshoppers. The sun started going down, and darkness slipped in over the pink light of the evening sun, slid through the trees with carbon-stained fingers, fell over the water and made inky splotches. In short time, through the limbs and leaves, you could see the sun swelling red like a big rubber ball, falling behind the world in slow motion. Finally, it was dead dark and the mosquitoes came out, big guys that could straddle a turkey flat-footed. They buzzed around our ears until we gave it up and got inside the tent and pulled the mosquito netting over the open front flaps. I took some bug spray from my camping bag, and we took turns spraying it on each other.

When we felt the tent was secure from mosquitoes, I slipped back out, got some camping gear out of the car, including a camping light, which I hung from a loop in the top of the tent. I got some cooking goods too. A frying pan, a couple pots, a Dutch oven and a coffeepot and a bag of Maxwell House coffee. I had a box with a bag of flour and a can of lard in it, sourdough starter my mom had prepared for me, pepper, salt, some odds and ends for frying up fish, which we didn't have. I had a container of water with a spout, and I brought that in too. I was only missing a TV set and a tall antenna to bring in programs from Shreveport.

Under the lantern light, Leonard started cleaning out the square of bricks with a little camp shovel. I took a hatchet and went looking for firewood.

The wood around the tent was damp, so I had to go into the woods a bit. I was able to find some thin pieces of fairly dried wood, and a couple of larger limbs I could bust open with an axe to get at the pith and use for fire starter. I also managed to acquire a few ticks on my balls, which I stealthily picked off outside the tent.

After I got the fire going, it was hot inside the tent, but the flap being opened helped. The wind made the mosquito net in the doorway tremble.

I used a bit of flour and the starter and stuck it together with lard, and used a bit of water to make it smooth. I decided not to use any eggs. I rolled the dough with my hands on a paper bag placed on the picnic table until I had a small, thin blanket of dough. I coated the dough with a filmy layer of lard, dropped the hot dogs onto it, and wrapped the dough around them. I coated the inside of the Dutch oven with lard and put the dough and hot dogs inside of it, set the lid down over it. I used the little camp shovel to make room in the firewood and ash and sat the oven in that, shoveled some of the burning coals on top of the lid. Leonard found a spot where he could set the coffeepot, and he got the water inside boiling and he put the grounds directly into the water, cowboy style.

When I thought it was done, I worked the lid off again, and set it aside. It smelled really good.

We cut some slices out of the dough, like it was a deep-dish pie, and put them on the sacks the supplies had been in. We sat at the picnic table and ate with our hands. Food eaten outdoors like that, cooked on a fire, seems to taste better to me. Maybe it's psychological, but it sure was fine.

The smoke inside the tent was annoying, and we fanned out the smoke and spread the coals inside the brick square, then rolled out our sleeping bags. We put one on each side of the table, on the concrete benches. It was a little narrow, but it worked well enough and made us less worried about snakes. We stretched out and lay in the dark, except for a little red glow that came from the brick fire pit. The air smelled of burnt wood and the remains of our supper.

"Trudy, you're officially divorced from her?"

"Yep. Got my papers when I was in the can."

"I don't want to shit on sacred memories, Hap, but she's a neurotic do-gooder that's mainly doing herself good. She's an idealist without a real agenda. She's bad for you, buddy."

"I know. But I miss her. I tell you, right now, knowing all that, I'd take her back in a heartbeat. I love her, man."

"You want to fuck her. Not the same thing."

"That isn't it."

"I don't know. You're pretty pussy-trained. I work on the other side of the fence, and that can train you too, the old wiener craving, but I got to think that pussy for you must be powerful stuff."

"It's pretty powerful, but that isn't it. I really love her."

"Don't matter how you feel, she's got to feel the same, and she don't."

"Thanks for the reminder."

"Just trying to talk straight to you."

"I know. I don't have to like it, though."

"Thing is, what's true is going to be true no matter what. When you were out of sight, you were pretty much out of mind, except for her having an address for the divorce papers."

"Don't keep boosting my confidence. I might get the big head. Shit. You know a lot about me, for being in Nam."

"I got your letters. You wrote a lot of them. It was like you were my mother."

"Prison gives you a lot of free time."

"Let's change the subject. We used to box, and you showed me some of the other stuff you learned, the martial arts stuff. I got some more of that in the army, though the hand-to-hand stuff they teach you is mostly shit. I think we should start practicing, doing some sparring and stuff."

"We can do that. I want to do that."

"I need a job too."

"We can go see if there's a job at the aluminum chair plant. Go together."

"Yeah. That's good. Been my life's ambition, to make fucking aluminum chairs."

We talked awhile longer, and then grew silent. The night sounds from outside grew, a chorus of insects and frogs, and we could hear the water running fast and gurgling below the high bank. The glow from the fire pit was gone and the cool air blew through the mosquito netting and we were comfortable in there.

In the morning I awoke early, before the crack of dawn, went outside and sat in one of the lawn chairs near the bank. The air smelled sweet and fresh from yesterday's rain. I had brought my rod and reel out with me, and I put an artificial bait on it by feel.

When first light showed yellow behind me and fell warm on my shoulders, I cast my line out into the water, which, though still moving fast, was not rushing as before.

I sat there and, bathed in the daylight, saw that the trees on the other side of the river were filled with black birds, almost more birds than leaves it seemed, and as the sun continued to rise behind me, and the sky strained out the purple and let in the blue, the birds suddenly took to the sky with a burst of wings and a squawking of voice.

A fish hit my line. I reeled it in. It was a small bass. I took it off the hook and ran a string through its gills, dropped the fish in the water and tied the end of the string to my chair.

I cast again, and almost immediately another bass hit, and in short time I had four of them. None of them were big, but they were all eating size.

I pulled them out of the water and off the string, used my pocketknife to gut them. I rinsed them in the river, took them up to the tent. When I pushed through the mosquito net, Leonard sat up.

"That's the first real night's sleep I've had. Didn't dream guts and blood and all that shit. Didn't see that fucker on the bicycle. It was like I was innocent and had never borrowed money."

"I slept good too," I said. "I woke up, thought for a brief moment I was still in Leavenworth, then felt overwhelmingly happy when I knew I wasn't."

Leonard pulled back the sleeping bag, got out of it, and began to slip on his pants. "I see you got a few fish. Go to the store?"

"Without you out there they been biting. We're having fried eggs and fish for breakfast."

"Sounds good."

Leonard went out and gathered wood, using the hatchet. When we got the fire going well, I made some flat bread, fried the eggs and fish. I made the coffee this time, strained the grounds through a cloth. It wasn't great coffee, but at least there weren't any grounds to chew on.

When we finished eating, without really talking about it, operating with that one mind we seemed to share, we packed up everything and drove away. We rolled our windows down and felt the cool morning air come in. We could smell the green of the woods and the wet of the river, and then we were on the little road out. "You know, I'd be lying there in the jungle," Leonard said, "and I could hear people praying, but I didn't pray, because, like you, I'm not a believer. I felt to even think about it was silly, as I didn't believe in God. But I damn sure believed in hope then, because that's all I had to believe in, except being ready. So, I always tried to be ready. I had to be ready every minute, every second out there. Last night, I wasn't ready. I wasn't cautious. It felt good to not be ready, to just sleep. I find you irritating, but soothing at the same time."

"I guess I'm supposed to believe there's a compliment

in that. Thing was, in prison, in my cell, I was all right, I felt fine there. It's when we went outside on the yard, or when we went to eat, all of us near one another, that's when I felt worried. That's when I was cranked up and ready, every fucking minute, especially after seeing that stabbing right in front of me. When I was in the cell, I was fine. I didn't have a bunk mate. It was just me. I had some books there, and I read a lot. I exercised in my cell, slept there, dreamed there, and confining as it was, I felt better and safer behind those bars than out on the concrete. When I left prison, got home, I didn't sleep well. I could be in my bed in my parents' house, and I'd feel like someone was behind me. But last night. It was fantastic."

"That's because I was there, big boy."

"Maybe."

We drove on, heading toward where Leonard would stay with his uncle, provided his uncle would let him, and then I would go home. I would cross the Sabine Bridge with its high water, sinking down now, finding its place between the shores, and I would go to bed tonight after a warm glass of milk. Leonard wouldn't be near. We wouldn't be able to talk and joke or fish. That concerned me a little.

Leonard made me promise that before bed we would go out and look at the North Star, and we'd know we were both doing it, even if not at that same moment. That was our connection. We were both home from the war and from prison, and we told ourselves we'd be fine, and we should look at that North Star every night as a way of feeling connected.

"Don't forget," Leonard said.

I didn't forget. I did just that for a lot of nights that followed, looking up at that North Star, knowing my brother was looking too, and that we were star companions.

Sometime later, when I finally saw Leonard again. I told him how I had done what he suggested, and how fine it made me feel, and what a good idea it was.

"Oh, yeah," Leonard said. "I remember now. I forgot about it."

GOOD EATS:
THE RECIPES OF HAP AND LEONARD

KASEY LANSDALE

HAP'S DISCLAIMER: These are the recipes as I remember them from my youth. Some of them handed down, some of them original, and some I can't remember. Feel free to experiment, and don't take every direction to heart. (Except when I specifically tell you to take something to heart. Ice water means ice water, by golly.) Also, since you're rich enough to buy this book, I'm going to assume you're rich enough to have an electric stove too. So everything will be presented to you as though that were true.

OF MICE AND MINESTRONE

As seen in "The Kitchen"

HC's Iced Tea

I decided it might be best to ease you in slow. Like training wheels on a bicycle, see if you can get yourself a batch of iced tea together without putting an eye out before we move on to something more lavish.

> **Water**
> 3–4 **tea bags** (black tea is my preference)
> **Lemon**
> **Ice**
> **Sugar** (optional)

Boil some water on the stove then turn off the heat. Toss the tea bags in the water. Remember, the number of bags can be subjective depending on how much water you boiled, which is based on how much tea you want. Let the tea bags steep for about 4 minutes. Don't let it sit too much longer than that or your tea will turn more bitter than Uncle Chester about having a gay nephew. Pour it in a jug full of ice. Add some lemon or sugar if you feel so inclined. Pour it into a big glass and enjoy.

Mama's Pecan Bread

There was one major rule in the house when pecan bread was on the menu. Absolutely no running or slamming doors inside, lest you cause the bread to fall. I never did know if this really made a difference, but I wasn't trying to find out. I could see it now, the headline would read something like "Local boy accused of ruining pecan bread found snatched up, hide tanned. Mother questions where things went so wrong." My folks weren't big on whippings, and I wanted to keep it that way.

> 1 cup **sugar**
> 1 cup **brown sugar**
> 4 **eggs**
> 1 cup **vegetable oil**
> 1½ cups **self-rising flour**
> 1 tsp **vanilla**
> 2 cups chopped-up **pecans** (better when they're from the trees out back)

Turn on your oven and get it warmed up to 350 degrees. Spray a 9x13 casserole dish with some Pam, or get a stick of butter and rub it inside the pan. Get a glass bowl and mix together the sugar, brown sugar, eggs, and oil. Stir with a fork or whisk. Next, add the flour and the vanilla. Now stir that up until everything is smooth, with a nice golden color. Once your bowl looks like a wheat field, add your pecans.

Pay attention now, do not add all of them.

You want to save some, about a half a cup, to put on the top. So help me if you add all the pecans at once, you're on your own. Stir it around until the pecans are mixed in, then spoon it into the greased dish. Spread it out evenly, *then* add the remaining pecans. It should look pretty covered, like ants on a picnic.

Bake that sucker for about a half hour, then let it cool. Cut it up into squares and marvel at the wonder that is Mama's Pecan Bread. And remember, no running in the house.

Mimi's Pie Crust

My honest opinion: it's wrong to buy your pie crust already made. It's like cheating at cards. You might get away with it, but that don't make it right. And besides, there's nothing like your own flaky disc of deliciousness that you put your own blood, sweat, and tears into. Metaphorically of course. Just ask yourself, what could possibly go wrong? I ask Leonard that all the time. Though come to think of it, he usually answers with "Do you know us?" Ignore him; he ain't always right.

    1½ cups **Crisco** (vegetable shortening)
    3 cups **all purpose flour**

1 **egg**
Salt
1 tbsp **white vinegar**
1 **egg**
5 tbsp **ice cold water** (that doesn't mean
run the tap to cold)
Salt

First things first, and let's just get this out of the way. You can't use butter. You sure as hell can't use olive oil or some other fancy pants butter alternative. You *must* use Crisco. Lord forgive me for what I am doing to my arteries, but if you want a flaky and delicious pie crust, that's just what you have to do. Now, put the flour in a bowl and add the Crisco. I grew up with a girl who used to work the mules in the fields, plowing all day in the hot sun. She'd come home starving, would take a big old spoonful of Crisco and then dip it in sugar, and eat it straight. She died very young. I am not saying those two things are connected, but I'm not saying they ain't.

Anyway, find your pastry cutter (or two knives if you're able) and work that Crisco through the flour. Do this until there's no chunky bits in it. This part takes a little practice, but eventually you can see the texture and know it's ready. Take your egg and crack it into a different clean bowl. Grab you a fork and whip that egg like it stole something. Now pour it onto the flour mixture and add the cold water and vinegar. Add the salt. Mix it together lightly. Don't beat the tar out of it: the mixture is not your enemy. Take that ball of dough and wrap it in plastic. Put it in the ice box for about four hours (you can leave it until the next day even). If you are ready to make the pie now, separate the dough into manageable sections, and freeze it slightly flattened for 20–30 minutes.

*Side note: When you are ready to spread the dough out for baking, get a rolling pin and flour whatever hard surface you have. Sheet metal or butcher block is always perfect for this. You don't need an extravagant kitchen, just a hard surface you can spread some flour on. Roll out the dough from the center until it's flat. This is not your cousin's Play-Doh, so don't treat it as such. If you find the dough sticking to the pin as you roll, add a little more flour. You don't want it to be watery as you spread it out. I hope you don't have any prior engagements, 'cause getting the crust rolled out to the right size can take some time. Flour and flip as needed, and don't be afraid to get your mitts in there and firm up the edges when things start to crack. It ain't rocket science, just make it look like every other pie crust you've seen in your life. Roll the finished, flat dough up on your rolling pin like a scroll, then transfer it to your pie pan rather than trying to scrape it up off the countertop. You want the dough to fall over the edges of the pie pan when you finally put it in. Metal pie pans are the way to go, but you do what you have to do. Tuck the edges of the crust under and then get a fork and crimp around the perimeter. If you just can't imagine placing a pie down in front of your family that isn't one hundred percent aesthetically pleasing, you can always use your fingers to pinch the border in for that clover look. (If you're a bit on the ostentatious side, a spoon or tongs can work too.)

O'Reta's Chocolate Pie Filling

I don't know what people have against writing down recipes, but this is how I remember it from when I was a kid. I had to make a few tweaks here and there until the memory and the taste aligned, but this is as old-fashioned and Southern-style as a chocolate pie can be. Now when I make this pie, which is usually only around holiday time 'cause let's be honest, nobody's getting younger and, for certain, nobody's getting thinner, least not 'round here, I always think of Mama. There she'd be, in the kitchen making all kinds of goodies. When we finally got a television, I'd come home from wherever I'd been that day and she'd have her stories on in the background. You weren't to disturb her then. You could be on fire and it wouldn't matter, not until the end of the program. That woman, though, could make anything out of anything. She was the MacGyver of ingredients.

> 1 cup **evaporated milk**
> 3 tbsp **flour**
> 3 tbsp **unsweetened cocoa powder** (One day I'll tell you 'bout the brownies Mama used to make using this same powder)
> 1 cup **sugar**
> 3 **eggs**, separated
> 2 tsp **vanilla extract**

Go ahead and turn on your oven to 350 degrees. Whether you bought it at the store, or you made it yourself, get your pie crust ready. Put a saucepan on the stove, but don't turn it on yet. Don't want you burning the filling before we even get started. Combine the milk, flour, cocoa powder, sugar, egg yolks, and vanilla. Now you can turn it on to medium. This next part is super-important: whisk that mix like Zeus trying to start a hurricane. You got to keep that liquid moving. It has been said that if you stop stirring, not only will you end up with a too-thick pie filling, there will also be a voodoo curse that descends upon your family from now to eternity. Nobody wants a voodoo curse, trust me. Once that filling starts bubbling up, you can reduce the heat to a simmer, and let it cook until it thickens. It'll sneak up on you and be too thick if you don't pay attention. What you want is a pudding consistency. Some people use pudding as their filling in general, but those people are wrong. You should have your pie crust at the ready, and with the filling still hot and the right consistency, pour that liquid gold into the crust.

*Don't ignore me now. It's very important that the meringue goes on the pie while the chocolate filling is still super-hot. You need to seal this puppy like your life depends on it. If you have questions, refer over to the meringue recipe. If you still have questions, call your mom. You should call her anyway without me having to say as much. Act like an adult. That woman gave birth to you. Show a little respect. If Mama ain't around no more, bless her soul, call someone who you know would love to hear from you. Don't wait on me to tell you who it is. Take some responsibility. Anyway, after you seal the pie, let it cool at room temperature.

Uncle Chester's Meringue

> 4 **egg whites**
> ¼ cup **sugar,** ground extra fine
> ¼ teaspoon **cream of tartar** (Uncle Chester would say this is a white man's addition, but I like it.)

Leonard here . . . Wasn't no way I was gonna let Hap here tell y'all about my Uncle Chester's meringue recipe. Uncle Chester always told me the secret to good meringue was this: cold eggs. You gotta separate the eggs from the egg whites straight out of the icebox. Then you leave them alone and let them reach room temperature. Go read a book, do a puzzle, put on some Ernest Tubb. Whatever you have to do to give them enough alone time so that your meringue turns out "Chester-Ready."

Uncle Chester used to always say, "Let them sit if you wanna whip."

I never had the heart to tell him it wasn't a great rhyme.

While you're waiting, put your sugar in a blender and let it get real fine. It holds a lot better when the sugar is almost powdery. I don't recommend using powdered sugar though. There's a difference, is what I'm saying.

Once you're sure it's been long enough, pour the egg whites into a clean bowl that has been sitting in the icebox a few minutes. Listen to me when I say clean, 'cause I mean clean like baby Jesus is coming over for dinner kind of clean, and whip them until they are as glossy white as Hap's ass. Unlike Hap's ass, do not over-whip. Add the cream of tartar so the eggs will hold their shape. I don't remember seeing Chester use cream of tartar, but I know I haven't been able to make a chocolate meringue pie myself without it. Slowly add the sugar to the egg whites, about a tablespoon at a time.

Now, if you'll notice, Hap said before that it's very

important that the meringue goes on the pie while the chocolate filling is still super-hot! This is still true. Also as Hap said before, you need to seal the pie correctly. You can do so by taking your meringue all the way to the outer edges of the pie so that when it does shrink, it still covers all the filling. Trust me, nobody wants shrinkage. Uncle Chester taught me that early on about several things. This meringue can also be used on top of my namesake banana pudding.

**Now you have the crust, the filling, and the meringue recipes all at your disposal. Go forth, good luck, and Godspeed.

As seen in "Of Mice and Minestrone"

Kill Ya Dead Jalapeño Cornbread

I know some people like sweet yellow cornbread, and it's true that I've been known to indulge myself on some occasions. But real cornbread, the old style like Mama used to make, wasn't even called cornbread. It was known as "corn pone," and it sure didn't have no sugar.

Full disclosure though, I can't really tell you what the true difference is. Mind's been busy with other things, solving the world's problems and whatnot, but I know my mama was adamant that they were in fact, different.

Mark Twain even went so far as to suggest, "You tell me whar a man gits his corn pone, en I'll tell you what his 'pinions is." So as you can see, cornbread, or corn pone as it's known, has highly permeated Southern culture. It was Twain who also said, "The North thinks it knows how to make cornbread, but this is gross superstition."

> 1 tbsp **shortening**
> 1 cup **cornmeal**
> 1 slight tsp **salt**
> 1 cup **boiling water**
> **Jalapeños** to taste
> Ample **bacon grease** (Just use what's in
> the Folgers coffee can on the back of the
> stove.) *Ample can be defined as how
> much grease your body can handle today

It should be said that if you plan on using jalapeños straight off the vine, you should conduct a taste test on your batch to see what you're dealing with on the spice scale. Remember, without any sugar in the recipe, there's nothing to cut the heat from within. I suggest having a big glass of buttermilk nearby to keep those seeds from sneaking up on you, lest you find yourself yelling s'wanee and passing out right at the kitchen table.

Start off by melting the shortening in a heavy iron

skillet, then put the cornmeal and the salt in a different bowl. Use another pot on the back burner to get some water boiling. Take a cup of boiling water and pour it over the cornmeal and the salt. Believe me when I say it needs to be hotter than a billygoat with a blowtorch. Go ahead and add the melted shortening (and chopped jalapeños if you're using them) and stir it up with a long wooden spoon. Once things cool off, portion it out evenly into little cakes. Keep it sort of thick, don't flatten it out. We aren't making pancakes over here. Next, put you some bacon grease in the skillet, about ¼ of an inch, and turn the heat to medium. Let it get hot, then place the cakes in the skillet until they fry up brown. Should take five minutes or so, and for Pete's sake, don't forget to do both sides.

*Recommended with Death by Chili and Minnie's Minestrone.

Minnie's Minestrone Soup

To this day I still think of Minnie, especially when I hear the word "Minestrone." I think of how ashamed I was that I didn't stand up to Dash that first time. I also think that maybe I'd be laying next to Minnie if I had. I think too of my father, how in his own way, the best way he knew how, told me some things just ain't never going to be right in this world. That sometimes bad things happen to good, and bad, people, and life ain't always fair. How that feeling, that discovery, don't make you special, but part of a sad little club nobody wants to be a member of.

Making this soup, though, makes me smile. I smile knowing that Minnie was a fighter right up until the end. A cruel end that came too soon. That maybe, just maybe, meeting me, getting away once, even if only for a short time, made her stronger somehow. In the end, didn't help enough, but it's the only way I can make any sort of peace with what happened. I never did see Dash again, but I heard that he got liver cancer, and suffered right up until he died alone, penniless. I hoped it was true. So Minnie, here's for you.

> 1 tbsp **olive oil**
> 1 tbsp **butter**
> 2 large **carrots,** diced
> 1 medium **onion,** chopped
> 2 **celery ribs,** chopped
> 3 **garlic cloves,** minced
> 2 cans (14½ ounces) **chicken broth**
> 2 cans (8 ounces) no-salt-added **tomato sauce**
> (I'm trying to watch my girlish figure.)
> 1 can (16 ounces) **kidney beans,** rinsed
> and drained
> 1 can (14½ ounces) diced **tomatoes,** und-
> rained

1½ cups shredded **spinach**

1 tbsp dried **basil**

1½ tsp dried **parsley** flakes

1 tsp dried **oregano**

½ tsp **pepper**

1 whole shredded or sliced **zucchini**

1 cup uncooked **elbow macaroni** (or whatever you have left in the cabinet)

*Poisoned rats optional.

Find you a big saucepan (like the state of Texas big,) and put the butter and oil in it. Then, sauté your carrots, onion, and your celery. Next, add the garlic. Let that cook for about another minute, then add everything but your noodles. Cook that until it boils up, stir it, then reduce the heat. Put a lid on it, and let it simmer for about 15 minutes. If you're ready to eat it, add the macaroni and cook without the lid on another 7 or so minutes. Basically, just keep your eyes on things, and if the pasta looks done, and the veggies look done, it's safe to assume that they are. You can be sure by poking around in there with a fork, or some other pointy object, to make sure things are tender.

There's a lot of stuff that goes into this soup, but there's not really that much to it as far as the cooking process. Also, it's sort of a kitchen sink recipe. In other words, if you've got it, go ahead and toss it in there. If you prefer fresh tomatoes, for example, or low-sodium options, that's all you. I know some people add more vegetables, or chickpeas, or they sub the macaroni with another type of pasta. If you're a vegetarian, you can use vegetable broth instead of chicken. There's lots you can do with this recipe to make it your own. Spice it up or tone it down as you see fit. You can also add grated parmesan cheese when you're ready to serve, but I wouldn't do it if you plan to freeze it (see below).

*This makes a huge helping of soup. If you plan to freeze some for later, cook the pasta another time and add it in when you're ready to eat it so that it won't get gooey. Also, let the soup cool down before you freeze it.

Mom's Mexican Mess

Mom started making what became known as "Mexican Mess" when one day at dinnertime, she realized she didn't have enough ingredients for one of the meals in her regular rotation. She had some ground beef leftover from our cow, Spare Ribs. (We named him that to keep reminding us he wasn't our pet, he was lunch.) She had some canned goods and a bag of chips, and with that, Mexican Mess was born. She started tossing everything together on the stove and created her signature "Mess." Because it was always a mishmash of things, there weren't really consistent measurements. This recipe continues to evolve over time, but my favorite iteration is as follows:

> 1 pound **hamburger meat** (easier when you don't know the cow personally)
>
> **Taco seasoning** (Buy a pouch of it at the market. This is my splurge and I won't feel guilty about it.)
>
> 1 can **whole kernel corn** (This we usually got from the neighbors in exchange for work Daddy did on the man's car. It typically arrived in a wooden basket, was usually still on the cob and in the husk. Nowadays, I like to buy it in a can or even a freezer bag, ready to go. If you use it from the can, drain it first.)
>
> 1 can **pinto beans** (You can buy them dry and soak them, but sometimes the Piggly Wiggly runs a special, and it's easier to just stock up at that time.)
>
> 1 can **Black beans** (This addition came about later, when black beans suddenly became a part of every American's consciousness. You can always substitute kidney beans, and no need to drain either if you're using from the can.)
>
> **Fritos** (If you don't have Fritos, which makes me question you and is a whole

'nother conversation, get some old tortillas and fry them until they're crispy, then rip them into strips.)

Jalapeños (From the pepper plant on the front porch. Hard to believe we got those little seeds to not only sprout up, but live through a number of scorching Texas summers.)

Shredded cheese, added on top to taste

*A great addition on the top of this mess pile is some Hit Ya So Hard Homemade Hot Sauce.

Toss what's left of poor Spare Ribs on the stove in a greased pan and cook the meat until it browns. Drain off the fat as best you can, then add the taco seasoning. After the seasoning cooks through, dump the corn and beans into the mix. Stir it up nice, and when the smell starts to permeate the kitchen, turn off the heat and scoop it into a bowl. You can even put the Fritos on the bottom of the bowl, or put a tortilla on a plate, scoop the mess into the tortilla and roll it up. Don't forget to add the jalapeños and cheese as desired. If you're watching your figure like Leonard and me have been lately, skip the chips and tortillas and just eat the mess as is with a fork. Comfort food at its finest.

Pop's Chocolate Shake

> ¾ cup **milk** (the fatty kind, none of that
> new age crap)
> ¼ cup **chocolate syrup** (have an affection
> for Hershey's)
> 1 tbsp **malted milk powder**
> 1½ cups **ice cream** (vanilla was Pop's favor-
> ite, chocolate is mine. You can use any kind
> you want 'cause you're grown.)
> **Whipped cream** (a dollop'll do you.)
> **Cherries** (1–3 per shake)

Over at the café they used to make the shakes pretty
simple-like. They would pour the milk, chocolate syrup,
malted milk powder, and ice cream all together in a blender and let it run until it was the right consistency: smooth
like mashed potatoes. Then, they would pour it into a tall
glass that had been stored in the freezer. Pop always got
his topped off with whipped cream and one cherry. Pop
wasn't a glutton. I, on the other, hand prefer mine with
three cherries. Tastes better with three, if you ask me. If
you happen to be making a birthday shake of some sort,
you can always add sprinkles.

OF MICE AND MINESTRONE

Bud's Warm Milk

This one should be pretty self-explanatory, but there's a few little tweaks you can do to make a nighttime glass of warm milk go from good to downright delicious. Now, Dad wasn't much into froufrou stuff, but every once in a while, he would warm up a glass of milk on the stove and add in some vanilla extract, nutmeg or cinnamon (cinnamon sticks if you're feeling fancy), and if the neighbors had dropped some off from their hives, fresh honey. You want to be sure you don't let the milk sit too long on the stove lest you end up with a scalded batch. And don't forget to stir the milk as it gets warm, 'cause nothing tastes worse than burnt milk. Okay that's not true, there's actually plenty things worse than burnt milk, but that doesn't make it taste any better.

As seen in "The Watering Shed"

Watering Shed Moonshine

After the Watering Shed got slapped with a few citations for distributing moonshine without a license, they quit making it in the bathtub, letting it ferment for weeks at a time, and started using the stove. Seemed like a novel idea, you ask me. Not being much of a drinker myself, I couldn't really taste the difference of that made in the tub and that on the stove. Either way, it all has a flavor about as subtle as rocket fuel.

Enough **cinnamon sticks** that is starts to smell like Christmas (about 10)
1 gallon **apple cider** (see below ★)
4 cups **apple juice** (You can buy it at any Piggly Wiggly.)
3 cups **brown sugar**
1 cup **white sugar**
Everclear, 190 proof (only illegal in some states)
(If you happen to be a Yankee—anywhere outside of Texas—you may need to find a high-proof alcohol alternative. You'll need a little over 3 cups.)
1 cup **rum**, 70 proof (Rumor has it that Shank uses Captain Morgan, and has even used up to 2 cups per batch instead of 1.)

And gather up 12-ish **Mason jars** and their lids from whatever jams you and your cousins have finished off.

★Easy way to make apple cider:

1/3 bushel fresh Delicious **apples**

Clean the apples and cut out any rough spots. Leave the skins, no need to make extra work for yourself. Quarter them and toss them in the blender until they look like applesauce. Get you a cheesecloth, and place that mush on top of it. With the cloth over a bowl, start squeezing like you're milking a goat. There. Fresh apple cider.

Making the shine:

Take the sticks (cinnamon, that is), apple cider, and apple juice, and put them together in a big pot on a stove or over a campfire and bring it to a mild simmer. When it looks like Leonard's bathwater, add in the sugars and stir 5 to 10 minutes, until the sugar is gone. Turn off the heat and go find you a book. Read that book, then come back and check on the shine. Now that the mixture is at room temperature or slightly below, stir in the Everclear and the rum. (If you skip reading the book and go straight to adding the booze, it'll burn off some of the alcohol.) Now you can pour that soul-scorching nectar into a Mason jar, and if you're feeling fancy, you can add a cinnamon stick inside there too. Pinkies up.

Shank's Cherry Bombs

The Watering Shed doesn't exactly scream variety, but Shank always has something in the back just in case someone ventures out to his establishment with a hankering for something a little more exotic. Disclaimer: Cherry Bombs have been known to cause vomiting, dehydration, pregnancy, and death.

> "Leftover" **Everclear** from the moonshine
> Jar of **Maraschino cherries** (Piggly Wiggly is still your best best.)

Drain the jar of cherries, and once the juice is out, replace said juice with the Everclear and let them soak a few days in the icebox. Can be served with soda or eaten alone. Be careful though: eat too many, you might be visiting Philip sooner than later.

As seen in "Sparring Partner"

Leonard's Banana Pudding

Ain't a soul alive don't know that vanilla cookies is Leonard's favorite. I've seen him throw hands over someone just looking at his cookies. I can't say as I blame him; they are pretty great. No matter how broke we may be, he's always got to get the brand-name vanilla wafers. Leonard's funny about that. They taste the same to me, but he swears up and down there's a difference, and who am I to come between a man and his cookies? So with all this in mind, it's no wonder Leonard's favorite dessert is banana pudding. If we poured Dr Pepper on top we might just be uncovering his holy grail. Though I don't recommend you pour anything on top of the banana pudding other than caramel sauce. That's a little decadent if you ask me, but so long as it ain't a soft drink I guess that's okay. One great thing about banana pudding is it doesn't take long to make. So, if it turns out you got kin dropping by in an hour, no need to panic, and you likely already have everything you need.

> 4 tbsp **all purpose flour**
> 1½ cups **sugar**
> Pinch of **salt**
> 3 **egg yolks** (You can save these egg whites to put towards the Meringue.)
> 3 cups **milk**
> 1 tsp **vanilla extract**
> Box of **Nilla Wafers** (from anywhere but Leonard's pantry)
> 6 **bananas**

Fire up the stove to 325 degrees and let it heat up. Grab you a saucepan with some weight behind it, and put in the flour, sugar, and salt. In a different bowl, beat three egg yolks like they owe you money, and add the milk to the same bowl with the eggs. Pour that mixture into the saucepan and then cook over medium heat, stirring constantly, like it's your full-time job, until everything is smooth as a baby's bottom. Take the pan off the heat and stir in the vanilla. Once that pudding mixture has cooled, arrange some of the vanilla wafers on the bottom of a glass dish. Slice up your bananas, and place some of them on top of the wafers. Then pour about 1/3 of the pudding over the layers and repeat, ending with the cookies on top. If you want to add meringue, then by all means. Who am I to stop you?

Hit Ya So Hard Homemade Hot Sauce

Pound of fresh **chiles** (Serrano, poblano, chiltepin, jalapeño, habanero . . . you get the point. You can stick to one or experiment with a mix. I usually just use whatever I managed to grow this season that the bugs ain't gotten into.)
1½ tbsp minced **garlic**
½ cup diced **onion**
2 tbsp **salt**
1½ cups **white vinegar**
I have also used smoked salt, and a dash of

paprika a time or two, but neither of those
things are necessary, and it's been reported that some people don't like the cross-up
of that many tastes for their hot sauce. To
each his own, as they say.

Toss the chiles, garlic, and the diced onion, along with
the salt, into the blender until it's the consistency of a
chunky tomato sauce. Pour the puree into a Mason jar,
cover loosely, and leave it out on the countertop overnight. The next day, add your vinegar, then stir. Don't
go to town on it, just make sure it permeates the sauce.
Now, this is where you just have to wait. You let it sit on
that same counter (okay, it doesn't have to be the same
counter) and leave it there for up to a week. The longer
it sits, the more concentrated it'll be. Once enough time
has passed, pour that mixture back into the blender and
let it run until smooth. Pour it back into that Mason jar
and store it in the icebox. Technically, it will last you
four months, but I think we both know it'll never make
it that long. If you pull it out and it looks weird, don't
worry, it's supposed to separate. Make sure that lid's on
there tighter than a hair in a biscuit, and shake it up until it smooths back out. Can be enjoyed with everything.
Seriously, you can add hot sauce to anything. Can and
should are not the same, but nonetheless.

GOOD EATS: THE RECIPES OF HAP AND LEONARD

As seen in "The Sabine Was High"

Hap's Hard Eggs and Cheese

> 2–3 **eggs** (depending on how hungry you
> are; that's sort of up to you)
> **Shredded cheese** (same thing)
> **Salt** and **pepper** to taste
> **Cayenne pepper** (optional)

There's no great magic happening here, and this recipe came about one day by mistake. I was just getting breakfast ready on the stove when Leonard came knocking on the door, distracting me from what I was doing. I went to answer, we got to talking, and damned if I hadn't forgotten about my breakfast. By the time he went on and I made it back to what I was doing, there they were. Hard eggs. All you got to do is put some Pam cooking spray or some kind of oil in your pan and let it get hot. Now crack your eggs into the pan. I know most people would recommend doing it in a bowl first, stirring everything together, but I like to cut out the extra dirty dishes. It'll be fine. Besides, an old trick I learned to get eggshells out of anything is the get a spoon, run it under the water faucet, and eggshells will stick to that wet spoon. You're welcome.

So, as I was saying, crack your eggs into the pan and let them sit. That's about all there is to it. If your best friend comes knocking at the door with news, don't be shy about it. Go on, answer the door. When you come back, those eggs should be getting nice and hard. You can let them keep cooking, and then add cheese and seasoning as desired. If you're tired of waiting, you can scramble up what remains and then add the cheese and seasoning. Either way, the eggs will be delicious and not much labor involved on this one. When they look right to you, scrape those suckers onto a plate and enjoy. Don't forget you can add some homemade hot sauce too.

Brer Rabbit Cookies

Mama started baking these cookies during the sugar rationing of World War Two, and never stopped. To me, brother rabbit was just that. A rabbit. I'd seen him fight a baby made of tar as a kid, which at the time I accepted as plausible and factual. As I got older, it became clear to me that old Brer Rabbit was the cause of most of his own troubles. He was cunning, all right, but only after he put himself in a piss-poor situation to begin with.

Don't get me started on Walt Disney. Wasn't until I was older and heard about Uncle Remus, I realized that Disney had pulled another fast one on me. Another, you might ask? That's right, I found out the hard way that Mickey was a guy in a suit. I don't want to talk about it.

Anyhow, I digress. If you're rationing sugar for one reason or another, or you just like the taste of molasses, these cookies are for you. This is the recipe exactly as I remember it on the back of the bottle.

¾ cup **shortening**

1 cup **sugar**

1 large **egg** (I'm serious about it being large, not giant.)

¼ cup **unsulphured molasses**

2 cups **flour**

2 tsp **baking soda**

½ tsp **clove**

½ tsp **ginger**

1 tsp **cinnamon**

½ tsp **salt**

Start by melting your shortening, then let it cool. Seems counterproductive I suppose, but stay with me here. Once things have cooled off, add your sugar, your egg, and then the star of the cookie show, your molasses. Remind me at another time to tell you about the first time I was offered a mole-ass cookie at Christmastime. Neither here nor there . . . Sift the rest of the ingredients together in a different bowl, and once combined, add them all together with the shortening mixture. Beat this mixture well. I mean really get in there. Now that it's all mixed up, let it chill a few hours, or leave it until tomorrow. When you're ready, take out the mix and form it into small balls. I'm gonna just keep plowing forward here . . . Roll this mixture in some extra sugar you have set aside (probably should have mentioned that up top) and place them on a greased cookie sheet a few inches apart. I probably should have also told you to preheat the oven to 375 degrees. The small ball thing threw me for a loop. Bake the cookies about 7 minutes. You're looking for light-as-a-cloud-like on the texture scale.

Doing all this cooking brings back many memories of my childhood. My parents always made sure I didn't do without, even if they did. So sometimes, when I make these cookies, I put a little spoonful of Brer Rabbit Molasses on a saucer and do something I remember seeing Dad do. He'd pour hot coffee on top of a glob of Brer Rabbit Syrup, (or "surp" as he would call it). Then he would wipe it up with a biscuit, piece of plain cornbread, or a slice of toast. Sometimes he'd add bacon. When you're broke, you get inventive, as you can tell from some of these recipes.

Death by Chili

Even though I didn't get a chance to tell y'all about some of my chili adventures in this collection, I thought it important to include this recipe, as it's the quintessential Hap Collins dish. How do you think I got Trudy, or Brett, or Florida? Wasn't just my boyish charm. This chili recipe is foolproof. I'm the living, breathing example of that. And so, I wanted to share this with you because if there's one thing Hap Collins knows a thing or two about, it's chili. Especially Bad Chili, which this is not. On that note, there will be zero debate about where the best chili is made. It's Texas. End of discussion. To make your own bowl of red, you'll need everything listed below, as well as some wet wipes and a roll of TUMS handy. You will thank me later. And don't go adding beans in there. That's just wrong. This is best served with Kill Ya Dead Jalapeño Cornbread.

Hamburger meat (a lot)
Steak strips (also a lot)
1–2 cups **water**
10 oz **tomato paste**
2 tsp **sugar**
4 tsp **chili powder**
10 **jalapeño peppers,** sliced
Dash of **cayenne**
Dash of **Tabasco sauce**
2 cloves **garlic,** minced
1 tbsp **olive oil**
3 ripe **tomatoes**
1 small **onion**

½ tsp **oregano**

1 tbsp **black pepper**

Pinch of **salt**

Ghost chili pepper (optional)

First, cook the hamburger meat and brown it, and then drain the grease. I'm not sure how much is a lot, but a lot. Take that cooked meat and put it in a big pot on the stove. Now get the steak and cut it into strips. Add the steak strips to the empty pan until they start to brown. Once the meat is the right temperature, put it on a cutting board and cut it into chunks. Then, add it to the pot.

Now here's where you have to pay attention, 'cause you don't want to make it too watery, this ain't the Sabine. Turn the heat to medium, add a cup of water, and about 10 ounces of tomato paste. Stir it up with a long wooden spoon. Keep stirring and put in the sugar, chili powder, and jalapeño peppers. If it seems too thick, add some more water. If it seems runny, add some more tomato paste (assuming you had some left in the can).

Full disclosure, I've seen some people use ketchup in a pinch. Now toss in the cayenne, Tabasco, and garlic. You are your own master, so if this don't seem right, adjust according to your own taste. Also, don't forget the oil. Lard is always an option, but I like olive oil. Add a tablespoon to grease the proverbial wheels. Again, you'll thank me later.

Take the fresh tomatoes, cut them up, and toss them

into the mix. Dice up a small onion and do the same. Add oregano, some pepper, and a pinch of salt. Let simmer a long damn time. When you think it's been long enough, let it simmer just a little bit more. You can add water as needed, but do so sparingly. When it comes time to eat, it should be just right. If it isn't, you may have followed the recipe too closely. You have only yourself to blame.

These recipes may change over time, but the comfort they provide, sometimes only in familiarity, remains the same.

There is one thing that will never change. As Leonard says, "I ain't having none of that pie they use whip cream on the top and not meringue, I'll tell you that."

From mine and Leonard's family to yours.

—Hap Collins

ACKNOWLEDGMENTS

I'd like to thank Rick Klaw for his editorship and friendship over the years, and thanks to my daughter, Kasey, for the recipes and for being so magnificent. And thanks to Karen, my wife, and Keith, my son, for always being so supportive. And thanks too to all the Hap and Leonard fans who have enjoyed their adventures over the years.

Joe R. Lansdale is the author of fifty novels and more than thirty short story collections. He has won multiple awards in crime, western, fantasy, and horror fiction. His work has appeared in films and in TV shows, such as *Hap and Leonard*, as well as scripted episodes of *Batman: The Animated Series*, *Son of Batman*, and many others. He lives in Nacogdoches, Texas, with his wife, Karen, and his pit bull, Nicky.

Musician, personality, writer, and editor **Kasey Lansdale** is the author of several short stories and novellas including the collection *Terror is Our Business*, co-authored with her father Joe R. Lansdale. She has appeared on The Sundance Channel, Animal Planet, IFC Channel, and others. Lansdale will be starring in a new reality TV show in early 2020 on USA Network.

New York Times bestselling author **Kathleen Kent**'s fourth book, titled *The Dime*, is a contemporary crime novel set in Dallas, nominated by both the Edgar Awards and the Nero Awards for Best Novel. The sequel to *The Dime*, titled *The Burn*, will be published in February 2020. Ms. Kent is also the author of three bestselling and award-winning historical novels, *The Heretic's Daughter*, *The Traitor's Wife*, and *The Outcasts*.